Penguin Books
Hotel de Dream

Emma Tennant grew up in the Borders of
Scotland. She now lives in London and has
published four novels: *The Colour of Rain*
(under the pseudonym of Catherine Aydy), *The
Time of the Crack* (published in Penguins as
The Crack), *The Last of the Country House
Murders* and *Hotel de Dream*. She has also
contributed to the *Listener*, the *New Statesman*,
Vogue and *7 Days*, and is the editor of the
literary newspaper *Bananas*. She has a son,
Matthew, and two daughters, Daisy and Rose.

D0755216

Emma Tennant

Hotel de Dream

Penguin Books

Penguin Books Ltd, Harmondsworth,
Middlesex, England
Penguin Books, 625 Madison Avenue,
New York, New York 10022, U.S.A.
Penguin Books Australia Ltd, Ringwood,
Victoria, Australia
Penguin Books Canada Ltd, 2801 John Street,
Markham, Ontario, Canada L3R 1B4
Penguin Books (N.Z.) Ltd, 182–190 Wairau Road,
Auckland 10, New Zealand

First published by Victor Gollancz Ltd 1976
Published in Penguin Books 1978

Copyright © Emma Tennant, 1976

Made and printed in Great Britain by
C. Nicholls & Company Ltd
Set in Monotype Times

For Julian and Marjorie

Mr Poynter dreamed he was in his City. It was square and white-walled and in the central park pollarded trees, each carrying the load of old English apple blossom permitted it once yearly, marched down combed paths towards the fountain. He was lying in his bed in the palace and, from the medley of Churchill speeches, Vera Lynn and snatches of ITMA, he could tell it was 8 a.m. and time to get up.

The sound of Mr Poynter's morning band became apparent in the palace square. Heels clicked and a nervous cough was suppressed with a handkerchief. The martial music began. Mr Poynter rose from his bed with the ease of a young man and went over to the chair where his uniform for the day had been laid out. From the concealed loudspeakers in the high chamber the voice of Field-Marshal Montgomery succeeded Tommy Handley. He stepped smartly into black trousers with a thin red piping, a jacket with gold epaulettes and five rows of medals, and pulled on a helmet from which a scarlet ostrich plume nodded and pranced as he made his way over to the public window. He opened it and stepped out. The crowd, some members of which looked bedraggled and resentful despite the fine weather and relentlessly blue sky that Mr Poynter ordained in his city, stood in a pale mass behind the military band. Hatless, their fair hair rippled in the breeze of Mr Poynter's choice – 58°F with a healthy nip in the air, suggesting recent frost and more to come at nightfall – like wind on a wheat field, he often thought. And the rows of blue eyes underneath as innocent as the sky.

A loud cheer went up, the band began to play from *Lohengrin*, Mr Poynter stood erect on the state balcony and looked out unsmiling at the scene.

The view from the balcony was Mr Poynter's masterpiece. The

7

city was set in rolling English pastureland, dotted here and there with Gothic spires, replicas of Stonehenge and gentle hills bearing the marks of Saxon parliaments: grassy benches that went down to trout pools, and great rook-laden trees that once provided shade for ancient kings. Despite the pleasant varied nature of the landscape, Mr Poynter had made sure that nothing interfered with the straight line of the horizon. Any burial mound, copse or hillock rising above that level had been lopped or cut down. The sky came down firmly to meet the land at an angle that set off to perfection the square walls of the city and the rectangular buildings within. Of course, as nothing can be perfect, and as Mr Poynter liked to show his belief in progress and reform, there was a ghetto in the city a mile or so south of the palace where the square marble and stone buildings had not yet been erected. Here the houses, which were constructed of papier mâché and cardboard, and stood on wheels like a complex and gigantic railway system, were ghastly and mean in appearance. At night, while Mr Poynter and his troops slept, these buildings zig-zagged madly about, running altogether into an unhygienic heap conducive to cholera and the elevation of barricades, or went to stand as forlorn ruins, garbage piled in their untended gardens; every morning after the *Lohengrin* and the hymn of thanksgiving, they were pushed back again into straight rows, some of their occupants arrested and others driven off to the Poynter Memorial Hospital in shiny white cars. The fetid smell of the place was demolished with disinfectant and a pine essence spray devised by Mr Poynter's wife.

Naturally, there were other uses for the ghetto. Mr Poynter's men and occasionally Mr Poynter himself, when affairs of state had been too pressing and the scent from the apple blossom crept under the doors of the palace, went down to these moving, unmanageable streets in search of pleasure. The brothels, run by old school friends of Mr Poynter's, catered to every taste. In the red light district, where a beautiful woman sat at every window, her golden hair shining in the candlelight and her arms folded pliantly in the pose ordained by Mr Poynter, whipping was common, and confinement for up to eight hours in a wooden box with spoonfuls of tapioca pudding and other nursery mush pushed in through a hole in the lid at the gratified customer, or – and this was Mr Poynter's speciality, and therefore copied widely in the ranks – the women would be attired in prep school outfits, their knees made up grazed and scuffed beneath the skimpy grey shorts, their hair hidden under little tricoloured caps and their feet unexpectedly large and clumsy in brown shoes with frayed and ink-stained laces. When Mr Poynter made one of his rare and exciting visits, boudoirs were transformed hastily into classrooms, a blackboard was hung over the standard reproduction of the Rokeby Venus, and it was on a bare wooden floor thick with chalk dust that Mr Poynter forgot the responsibilities of his position.

On this particular morning, having been caned the night before in the uncertain twilight zone by the girl who most closely resembled Sackers, the provocative bully of his childhood days, Mr Poynter knew he must make a visit of atonement to his wife and daughters. These ladies lived in a large mansion in the richest residential quarter of the city; sprinklers cast a permanent haze of fresh water over the lawns and around the windows of the house, as if, Mr Poynter sometimes thought, they lived in a perpetually refreshed dew drop; eunuchs served them at regular intervals with cups of coffee and what Mrs Poynter liked to call her little nibble. Inside, the house was painted in all the blues which have ever been associated with the Madonna - cerulean walls enclosed the matron and her two growing girls, azure ceilings and upholstery of velvet dyed to the colour of the startled irises of the Virgin on receipt of the Annunciation protected the female Poynters from any suggestion of impurity or evil. Between periwinkle sheets Mrs Poynter, who was seldom visited by her husband in the evenings, lay alone and counted laundry lists in her head. In the morning, when her husband called, she would be waiting for him in the blue and white majolica tiled hall, her smile forgiving and the necessary hint of reproach at the corners of her mouth similar to the slight nip in the air which Mr Poynter found so bracing an ingredient of the climate. Today, the bout with Sackers's understudy having been a particularly rigorous one, Mr Poynter determined he would go straight there and attend to other matters afterwards. The band stopped playing, the crowd

9

gave three huzzahs and dispersed, Mr Poynter saluted the horizon and went with a firm step back into the state chamber and out into the gold and white corridor.

As he went through the palace, brushing aside the A.D.C. with his usual list of requests and smiling benevolently at the bowing flunkeys arranged against the walls, walking out to the silent white Rolls which would waft him to his wife's house, Mr Poynter was aware that something somewhere had gone slightly wrong. He paused for a moment on the sparkling cobbles outside the entrance to the palace. The sun, perhaps, had got a little too hot: his shoulders itched under the epaulettes and the helmet felt strangely heavy: if it hadn't been for the presence of his troops and some of his subjects hurrying past on their way to work he would have removed it and gone bare-headed on his duty visit, but – and the crimson plume on top of his head which always seemed to agree with his pronouncements nodded vigorously as he climbed into the car – his breeze was still blowing and the temperature had never been known to change before. Perhaps he had gone beyond the boundary of guilt that he allowed himself after a visit to the District. No – he let out a naughty chuckle and the chauffeur's features relaxed as if he had just delivered one of his witticisms. That would be impossible. Probably it was his conscience; the ghetto still needed to be rebuilt; there was poverty and inequality, and he would be the first to admit it; later in the day, after receiving absolution from his wife, he would draft a new speech showing that he, like other highly respected leaders before him, could suffer at the wretchedness of human kind.

The car went at a dignified pace into the most exclusive quarter. Here and there an exiled dictator, stretched out with maps in a deck chair in the front garden of his quiet retreat, could be seen trying to struggle to his feet and salute as Mr Poynter passed. The birdsong, particularly loud and provided mostly by nearly extinct species brought into the city in great nets from the surrounding countryside, grew more intense. Dunkirk Avenue, at the end of which the Poynter residence was situated, came into sight, each garden laid out in a maze of topiary tanks and cannons, with regiments of red and yellow tulips flanking stately porticos. Mr Poynter felt his slight irritation disappear. The sun caught the play of water from the sprinklers on either side of him, so that he seemed to be moving within the spectrum of a rainbow. When he stepped from the car in front of his wife's house, a petal of cherry blossom landed on his tunic and he handed it to the chauffeur for disposal without the usual feeling of annoyance caused by these manifestations of nature. It was reassuring to see the white façade of his house at the end of the gravel path – a reminder that although you could be sure of nothing in the transitory ill-kept streets south of the palace, here all he believed in was intact and would always remain so.

Mr Poynter went up the path towards the windows and the soft blue rooms behind them with their cargo of innocent waiting women. The sprinklers splashing playfully on the lawns on either side of him made a triumphal arch of iridescent water. He reached the front doorstep and turned to look back at the great expanse of sward, the rectangular flowerbeds and the neat box hedge clipped to just the height convenient for Mrs Poynter to lean over and chat to a neighbour, had Mr Poynter thought of providing her with one. He stared at the grass; then frowned. On the lawn to the left of him, his particular favourite because of the ancient beech tree which dominated it and the sunken, centuries-old appearance of the grass, there ran a trail of mud, serpentine and about two feet wide. It trailed across the lawn in a haphazard fashion, as if a child had smeared it on with its fingers. Spurs clanking against his legs as he stooped, Mr Poynter descended from the step to examine it and frowned again. Sand – turned to mud by the shifting jets of water. There was no sand anywhere within the city and none outside, for Mr Poynter had a peculiar horror of the desert. Anger and perplexity brought a high colour to his face. He went in through the front door without further ceremony and shouted out his wife's name.

There was no sign of Hilda Poynter in the blue and white hall, nor of Clemmy and Alexandra, his daughters; but instead, a faint feeling of trouble, of a disturbance which Mr Poynter was quick to recognize and put down in his troops, but found himself unable to cope with for the moment, here. A shout of command rose to his lips, then died away. He strode through into the azure drawing-room and came to a full stop. His eyes went

11

rapidly round the room. The celestial ceiling, painted with suns and moons, hung above him as always. Velvet curtains and satin sofas and little tables carrying bowls of pot-pourri gave the normal, reassuring air of an English Edwardian country house. Hilda Poynter stood by the french window and at first glance she, too, seemed the same. The rich folds of her dress were arranged as Mr Poynter had ordained, her wimple was in place and, outlined against the square frame of the window and the calm garden beyond, she complemented the interior, giving it the Vermeer-like quality on which he insisted when he came home. But her face showed no tranquillity, her eyes had almost reverted to their natural brown, her cheekbones were taut and rigid. Mr Poynter came towards her with a mixture of concern and annoyance.

'Hilda! What is it? Something . . . bad seems to have happened out there.' He waved in the direction of the front of the house. Hilda Poynter smiled. Mr Poynter did not like her smile, it was wild and rather vulgar, showing more teeth than he had seen revealed in a long and happy married life together. Then tears began to fall. He shook her embroidered shoulders roughly.

'Look, Richard.' She pointed to the floor. On the area of dove-grey carpet by the French window lay a thin film of sand. She went up to it, then hung back, afraid to put her foot down in the substance.

'What on earth do you think you're doing with that stuff in here?' Poynter kicked at the sand and it flew at his immaculate boots, giving all at once a scruffy, dressed-up look to his general's uniform. Hilda Poynter wept and clung to his arm.

'A woman came in here, Richard, through there. Through the window. She was – enormous.'

Poynter turned and looked at his wife closely. His eyes flickered to the mother-of-pearl tray where a bottle of sweet sherry stood, in the event of callers. The glasses, upside down and highly polished, showed no sign of interference.

'An enormous woman,' he said in a flat tone. 'And did the girls see her, Hilda? And why, may I ask, should she bring this muck in with her?'

'She was naked.' Hilda Poynter gesticulated vaguely, her

puffed muslin sleeves flying out as she sketched a gigantic form in the air. 'Long hair . . . great legs . . . oh Richard, I can't tell you!'

'And she came in through the window.' Poynter sat down stiffly on a pristine sofa. 'She was covered in sand, then?'

'Yes, yes she was. She stood glaring at me a moment and then she ran off again over the lawn. I know I should have called the servants, but . . .' Here Hilda Poynter's voice tailed off. Her husband had a dead, remote look on his face, as if he had failed to hear what she had said or, if he had, had no intention of taking it seriously.

'Get the stuff cleared up then, my dear. And where are the girls? Has Clemmy made preparations for the ball tonight? Her dress, is that ready? And what about the flowers?'

At the mention of the ball, a blue light crept back into Hilda Poynter's eyes and she gave a tremulous smile.

'You think . . . I sort of dreamt it, Richard? I mean, perhaps the heat . . .' – (Mr Poynter's temperature did not suit his wife) – 'and all the excitement about tonight.' She gazed at him hopefully. Poynter rose and clicked his heels together. He looked down on his wife's smooth hair and patted the wimple, which rose like the horn of a unicorn from the back of her head.

'I expect so, Hilda.' He took his gold timepiece from the pocket of his uniform. 'You'll have to give the girls my love today, I'm afraid. Affairs of state.' He marched to the door, eyes averted from the sandy patch by the french window, and out into the hall. It was only when he reached the bright sunlight of the front garden that he became aware again of the condition of his boots; and he trotted at unaccustomed speed to the white Rolls and the waiting chauffeur.

The car carried Mr Poynter back to his palace. As he arrived in the main square and the piper on the roof began his slow, lugubrious welcome, a loud pounding sounded in Mr Poynter's ears. He looked around to see if target practice was going on in the artillery field by the west wing. There was no sign of anyone, but the pounding continued. The car stopped. Mr Poynter waited for the chauffeur to come round and let him out. He stretched out his hand as the door opened. It came down on a

13

sharp wooden surface, his head swam and dots appeared before his eyes.

'Tea, Mr Poynter.' The pounding died away, and Mrs Routledge's voice receded down the passage of the Westringham Hotel. Mr Poynter tossed uneasily in his bed, and woke.

'Tea, Miss Scranton.' A muffled hammering, on the door of the adjacent room, No. 22. Mr Poynter looked up at the stained curtains that let in, however hard he tweaked them together, the phlegm-coloured light of a London morning. At the patch of lino under the basin, chewed at the edges by the dog of a previous resident, the dark oblongs on the walls where mezzotints had hung before Mrs Routledge took them off to her brother-in-law to be sold. Tea! He struggled to a sitting position, his thin yellow legs came out of the bed and his feet went into slippers. Carefully, he dressed to go downstairs.

In Room 22, Jeannette Scranton dreamed she was on the edge of a vast beach. She was naked, and carried the big brown carpet-bag she took with her wherever she went – to staff-room meetings, downstairs to tea at the Westringham even – and she could tell from its weight that it contained its usual load of unmarked exercise books, exotic make-up that was seldom used, and the bundles of letters from the lecturer in linguistics who had once said that he was going to marry her. It was hot, and the sand was pleasantly firm beneath her bare feet. At the far end of the beach where groves of olive trees came down to the sea and a large, black cave stood like an open mouth against the blue sky, she could just make out what seemed to be a long hut and figures moving round it. She was relaxed – for the first time in years, she felt there was no particular hurry, no need to be in time for a lesson or to run for the bus before the rush hour started. She strolled along, the bag dangling against her thin haunches and the wavelets at her feet coming in and out gently as the sound of her own breath.

The walk to the hut seemed to take a long time, but Jeannette felt no fatigue. She was surprised, as she drew near, to see that the building was higher than she had expected: walls of plaited reeds went up to about twenty feet and supported a roof of olive branches, some freshly cut and with the leaves and small black fruit still on them. The women, too – and here Jeannette slowed her pace, and looked down at her own body to regain a sense of the proportion of things, appeared to be roughly double her height. They carried shields over great breasts that were thick with sand, and their legs, encrusted too so that they looked as if they had been dipped in gold dust, were as straight and solid as the trunks of trees. They had long, matted hair of a reddish

15

colour and large, bright eyes with which they appeared to relay messages to each other; Jeannette saw, even before she had come right up to them, that a glinting eye from one woman would cause another to go off into the grove behind the hut and return with branches, and that in the stream of light that flowed from their orbs there was complete understanding, love and sympathy. As far as Jeannette could see, there was no leader in the group, yet there was a sense of collective will-power as these creatures went about their daily tasks which suggested that they were preparing for something – a war, perhaps, or an important feast.

A handful of children, the same size as Jeannette in fact, but clearly not more than five or six years old, were collected at the entrance to the hut. They had what appeared to be blue paint smeared on their faces and were playing with an outsize ball made of plaited reed like the walls behind them. Jeannette saw they were all female. One of them pointed to her and took a step forward. Large black eyes looked into hers. Jeannette felt a message, inquisitive but not aggressive, sensed an optic nerve twitch in recognition, but nevertheless smiled politely and held out her hand.

'I'm Miss Scranton. Now any of you who want anything just come to me and explain your problem. Nothing to be frightened of, you know.' She twinkled and rummaged in her bag for sweets and coloured crayons she always carried with her at the beginning of a new term. The children's laughter beamed out of their eyes at her and she stood a moment at a loss, a red pentel grasped in her right hand and a boiled sweet half way out of the bag, ready for the conciliatory offering. One of the giantesses came up from behind the hut and stood staring at Jeannette. The others, she saw, were plunging into the water together as if at some prearranged signal: their brown buttocks rose and fell like the backs of dolphins in the sea, their hair streamed out behind them. Jeannette's interlocutor stood hands on hips, the sun glinting from her breastplate and turning it to a third, more monstrous eye. Jeannette looked up at the stern face. Her legs began to tremble beneath her. It seemed to her that she was being invited to join the group, but without ceremony or welcome. She thought of the rain-spattered days in the school playground at home, her room at the Westringham with the photograph of her mother on the chest of drawers, and the frown of pity on Mrs Routledge's face when she looked in at the paucity of Miss Scranton's possessions, and hesitated. There was something compelling about this invitation, a sense that she had been wandering unknown and unregarded in the wrong world and that she had come to her haven at last, quite by mistake and quite calmly, a haven she could have entered at any time but which for some reason was available to her for the first time now. All the same – she glanced at the cave and the rocky promontory that led out from it into the sea, the sporting women and the curious, open-faced children – how could she know she would be really safe here, that this wasn't yet another trap, like the time Miss Marchison had said they would be friends for ever and then turned on her after only a week, making her a figure of fun in the staff-room and avoiding her in the corridors as if she bore the mark of some unmentionable social leprosy?

The woman stretched out a hand and took hold of Jeannette's arm with thick fingers the colour of baked earth. She drew her down towards the sea and gave a playful push. Hearing the laughter of the other women ringing in her ears, Jeannette sank gratefully into warm salty water, and her bag floated away from her and down to the white pebbles of the sea bed. She began to swim, at first with the awkward breaststroke she herself taught in the school baths, and then with the rounded, rhythmic motions of the women. She dived and bobbed, rising to the surface to find their eyes shining out at her above the waves. They laughed, but without making any sound, and Jeannette's mouth slackened in response, the polite, defeated smile disappearing from her face and replaced by a great cavernous silent laugh, the sea slopping in and out of her mouth and her jaws and teeth aching. When the women, again after a message had flashed between them that was too quick for Jeannette to understand at once, began to make their way to the shore, she followed hastily. When they reached the beach, she rolled in the sand with them and like some survivor from a smaller, paler race, stood amongst their flanks awaiting the next signal.

The sun showed no sign of moving in the sky, but after what

seemed a few hours or a few days, Jeannette had become the mascot of the Amazons. They showed her a trophy that one of them, the tallest and most warlike of the troupe, had brought back from a recent foray to a distant land. It was square and transparent, and a picture of a pointed object was crudely painted on it, and Jeannette, with the faint memories that still remained in her of her previous life, tried to convey to them that this was where people in the other world placed ash when they had smoked, and that the pointed object was a building somewhere, she could not remember where, which was much admired and photographed. The women laughed and shrugged and replaced the glassy thing on a rough table in the long hut. They showed little curiosity about Jeannette, yet she felt she was there for some purpose and that they would make use of her one day on an important mission. While they indoctrinated her in their rituals of worship – at night, in the moonlight, around a tree stump garlanded with anemones and olive leaves, and prepared her for the day of mating by rubbing ointments on her body and hammering out her breastplate for her, Jeannette also felt that their idyllic life was coming to an end and that knowing it, they had ordered her to be sent to them.

The mating rite was in the hills, two days' walk from the women's hut. They told Jeannette that they would meet the men there from the far plains and drink and couple with them when the moon was full. Children would be conceived, the males left in the olive grove to die, and the females reared to swell their ranks. It was clear that the rite seldom took place, because a new atmosphere made itself felt as the time drew nearer: scorn and excitement showed on the women's faces and Jeannette felt some of her old nervousness returning, reminding her of the days when her mother had forced her to go to parties given by her friends for their children, and no one had asked her to dance. She started sleeping badly and would wake muttering in the night, the unaccustomed sounds from her throat bringing a powerful, comforting hand from a recumbent figure beside her. She knew, as the others seemed to, that this was to be the last of such encounters, and if she passed the test she would bear, as they all had, a child for the continuation of their race. As the day approached, her flesh tingled under the carapace of sand and she moved more freely, copying the wide confident stride of the women.

They set off in the early morning when the sea was still dark and the sun was touching the tops of the distant hills. They walked slowly, pausing to eat and drink and pray. After two nights, they had climbed through the scrub of the foothills and arrived on a plateau, protected like an amphitheatre by the mountains. They made camp and lit a fire. Because they were away from the sea, it was very quiet when night fell and Jeannette felt, for the first time since she had been with them, a frantic desire to hear the sound of a human voice. The women had stopped laughing, too, and their eyes were clouded and their faces solemn as they prepared themselves for the ritual.

The first sign of the men's coming was like wind in the trees on the surrounding hills. The women sat in a semicircle round the fire and looked up at the invisible horizon and then at each other. Jeannette heard horses and loud singing: pinpricks of light from the men's flares came in a straight line now across the plateau towards them. She shifted restlessly and a score of frowning eyes stilled her. The horses' hooves drummed on the parched grass.

'Tea, Miss Scranton.'

The hooves died away and the singing stopped. Jeannette turned in her bed and reached out a thin, white arm to the pile of school books on the bedside table. Next door, she heard Mr Poynter shuffle on to his lino mat and turn on the tap in his basin. She got out of bed and pulled her thin flannel dressing gown over her shoulders.

Miss Briggs dreamed she was at the Royal Garden Party. As always the Queen was quick to notice her in the crowd and, pushing past the officious and over-protective equerries, made her way through the throng of eagerly waiting subjects to reach Miss Briggs's side.

'The one person I wanted to see.' Her voice was so clear and distinctive that Miss Briggs often woke with a headache. 'We would like you to meet famous personalities today, concentrating on stars of screen and stage. Does that meet with your approval?'

Miss Briggs said it did. Last week, when Prince Philip had explained the workings of the internal combustion engine, and she had then been introduced to Crick and Watson, entertained by scandalous tales of the discovery of the Double Helix and chilled by the prognostications of futurologists, Miss Briggs had felt herself distinctly out of her depth. At tea later with Mrs Routledge in the lounge of the Westringham, she had thrown the topic of immunology casually into the conversation, only to be rewarded by a glassy stare from the other residents. Today she would be able to repeat the sayings of Sir John Gielgud, and with luck an amusing description of the two Hermiones. She smiled and bridled, and permitted herself to be taken by the hand and led to a marquee clearly reserved for the most important people. Red carpet was laid on the grass in front of it, and the entrance was done up to look like a theatre; from between the gold-fringed curtains actors and actresses could dimly be glimpsed sipping at glasses of champagne and raising canapés to their mouths.

'Lord Olivier,' the Queen said. 'Laurence, say hullo to Miss Briggs please.'

As the venerable actor bowed over her hand, Miss Briggs felt the familiar thrill. She waited for the Queen's next words – unaltered from dream to dream, summing up perennially her raison d'être – and simpered at the stooped head.

'A woman who is a true member of the human race. A woman who understands the pitfalls and evasions of life and has striven to overcome them. For this we have decorated her.'

The Queen's speech was done, and Lord Olivier looked up, his eyes moist with admiration. Last week the scientists had appeared bored with the reasons for Miss Briggs's elevated status in the land, and his response – but how could one expect anything else from a man who was the living embodiment of Shakespeare, the greatest of humanists – came as a relief. Sometimes, towards the end of the Garden Party when the Queen and Miss Briggs had done their duty, they discussed together in a whisper the unpleasantness of the world today: the relentless belief in growth and science and the fading away of all the traditional values. Secretly they planned to restore a sense of meaning to life, a world where promises were kept and God was worshipped. They both knew that a hard task lay ahead of them. But the Queen would have been unable to achieve anything without Miss Briggs, who was her adviser from the common people, and Miss Briggs would certainly have found her self-appointed mission harder without the Queen.

'You'll find none of the new young playwrights in there,' the Queen assured Miss Briggs as she seemed to falter at the entrance to the tent. 'I didn't invite them. I hope I did right?'

Miss Briggs nodded approval, although she felt a slight sense of disappointment. Often she had constructed the speech of admonition she would deal out to those who showed an England where defeat, poverty and apathy reigned.

'I'd love to meet the actress who was so brilliant in the Ibsen season,' she said graciously. 'I did find that most enjoyable, your Majesty.' (At the same time, she had to admit that Ibsen could be grim; but he had been dead a long time and was therefore respectable. If he were writing now, she very much doubted that she would advise the Royal Family to have him at their parties.)

'Of course you shall. We'll save the musicals to the last as a special treat, I thought.' The Queen gave a girlish laugh and Miss Briggs turned a benevolent smile on her. Many times, if the dream went on long enough, she and her monarch sat down in the private viewing theatre in the Palace and watched *The Sound of Music* just one more time. But now, with the rows of anxious thespian faces peering out from inside the tent, there were reassuring words to murmur and the message of the Silent Revolution to pass on. Miss Briggs stepped in, and a line was quickly formed.

'This is Miss Briggs.' The famous names bowed and curtsied with reverence and Miss Briggs's smile went unchanging from one to the other.

'We can count on you, I have no doubt, to stand firm by your country and your monarch when the troubles come?'

The actors muttered their assent. The Queen fluttered behind Miss Briggs, opening and shutting her handbag and pulling out from time to time a diamond star which was then pinned by an attendant equerry to the lapel of a particularly deserving guest. Miss Briggs thought of the occasion of her own decoration: the magnificent stateroom, the fanfare of trumpets, the Queen's children arranged on the dais beneath her; and was glad to see that today's ceremony would be relatively minor. There had been a stab of jealousy a couple of weeks ago, when an eminent biographer had received the full treatment in the stateroom, and the Queen had been punished for it afterwards, submitting to sulks and coldness from Miss Briggs. There had been mention of an even higher order as compensation for this disappointing event: Miss Briggs wondered, as she gave her low, thrilled laugh in response to Miss Gingold's jest, whether it might not possibly be later this afternoon. The Queen seemed definitely casual in the way she was handing out the diamond stars, as if something more important lay ahead. Miss Briggs determined to stay asleep right through morning tea if necessary, to find out – it would be too cruel to have to wait until tomorrow night for this.

'Only to say how much I have enjoyed meeting you all,' Miss Briggs concluded as she relinquished Miss Gingold's hand and shot one of her special smiles into the eyes of Sir John. His diamond star glittered back at her and she lifted a token glass of champagne. Alcohol had never agreed with her, and one morning, after a Ball to celebrate the engagement of Princess Anne, she had

22

been hung over all day, Mrs Routledge suspicious and coming into her room at odd times to check on hidden bottles.

'The Queen and I will now go and meet some of the other – and I'm sure you'll agree just as interesting – visitors to this lovely Garden Party. No doubt I will see you all soon on the stage, though whether I shall recognize you or not is another matter!'

Polite laughter rippled round the tent, and Miss Briggs went smoothly into the mixture of rain and sun which always seemed to prevail at these occasions, so that one half of the guests were permanently under black umbrellas and the other half, in floral dresses and hats, strolled on the bright paths without need of protection. The Queen followed; and engulfed by the sudden shower her presence invariably made manifest, they ran through the crowd to the little pavilion to which the less important visitors were brought.

'I've something I want to tell you,' the Queen said as they ran. They reached the pavilion, and sank down on gilt chairs under the domed roof, which was made of shells and designed by Miss Briggs herself. 'I want you to come to the stateroom when this is all over. I think you may be a little surprised.'

Miss Briggs dabbed the rain from her face with a lace handkerchief. Gratitude and a sense of the proper esteem in which she was held made her cheeks wet again and she blew her nose loudly.

'In fact,' the Queen whispered as she looked out on the line of shuffling guests, the bobbing umbrellas going off down the path as far as the eye could see, 'I think we might make a run for it now, don't you?'

Miss Briggs experienced that sense of near-ecstasy which came to her when the divine, magical powers of her monarch were put into operation. The formal gardens and queuing, hopeful subjects became a blur, a pink dissolve; her heart fluttered and then calmed itself, and when the rushing sound in her ears had abated she was smiling still, sitting bolt upright as she had been in the pavilion, except that she and the Queen were seated in the stateroom and she was on the great throne, a purple canopy above her head and an orb and sceptre in either hand.

'My intention is to hand the kingdom over to you, Miss Briggs.'

The Queen was at her feet, on the steps of the throne. She had removed her hat and looked small and vulnerable; Miss Briggs suppressed another wave of emotion and touched her lightly on the shoulder with the sceptre.

'But where will you go, my dear? I had thought to be a Dame, I must admit, but this –'

'We are emigrating.' The Queen's voice was soft and full of sadness. Miss Briggs sighed in sympathy.

'I believe the Australian landscape is most interesting,' she remarked by way of encouragement to the stooped figure beneath her. 'And the lyre bird can make a most rewarding pet.'

'We're not going to Australia. It's – it's Connecticut, as a matter of fact.'

'Connecticut?'

'A little village at the foot of the nuclear power station. You see, Miss Briggs, when the world goes we want to be the first. You would appreciate that, of course.'

'Of course.' Miss Briggs frowned as she murmured her assent. 'But – is the world going, your Majesty?'

'A small villa, but quite charming I believe.' The Queen swivelled on the richly carpeted step. She waved vaguely at the walls of the stateroom, where the prize pieces from her famous art collection shone dimly under gold-shaded lights. 'Look what's happened, Miss Briggs. Overnight. When we woke this morning . . . we will take some of the pictures with us, naturally, but there is no time to lose.'

Miss Briggs rummaged for her glasses under the ermine cape which had sprouted round her shoulders as the Queen spoke. She gazed at the great oils, the Van Dycks and the Turners and the Titians which she had so often revered on her previous visits to the stateroom. Then she let out a low moan of fear and surprise. The Queen nodded her head and leaned back against the dais, her eyes closed.

Each picture had undergone an unmistakable change. Some had suffered crude alterations, others – and this was even more ghastly – showed only subtle traces of the subject which someone (some practical joker presumably, in the worst of taste) had insisted on depicting in every canvas. Rubens beauties ascended to

24

the heavens on a mushroom cloud of palest, poisonous blue. The kings and dukes of the past, still astride their proud mounts, were in the most part faceless, though some, and at these Miss Briggs had to look away, gripped by nausea, had long aristocratic noses deformed by radioactivity and tapering fingers bunched into crude, mutant parodies of hands. The Turners, only yesterday the gems of the Royal collection, fine wild sprays of steam and mist and water seen through a haze of sun, showed only the final disaster in its various forms. Black, destroying clouds raged over grey skies. Transformed by nuclear gases, quiet Sussex parklands stood defoliated and bare, dead and dying deer grouped about the edge of a metallic lake. The Gainsborough ladies, stripped of their fine gowns in the holocaust, sat naked and shrivelled in their bowers and drawing-rooms. Miss Briggs shuddered and covered her eyes.

'There won't be enough room to take many with us,' the Queen said. Her tone was flat and dry, as if she had already prepared for her end in the little chalet by the power station. 'But at least they'll be in place there. Don't you agree?'

For the first time, Miss Briggs felt a surge of rebellion against her monarch rise up inside her. She rose, adjusting the heavy crown on her head with a shaking hand.

'And I am to be left to reign here,' she said coldly.

The Queen gave an uncharacteristic giggle. It crossed Miss Briggs's mind that she, too, might have been affected by the wicked and anonymous night-artist.

'Let the hard reign fall!' Serious again after her pun, the Queen rose and climbed the steps to kiss Miss Briggs on the cheek.

'Who can say how long you will have, my dear Miss Briggs? Enjoy it while you can!' Her face grew indistinct, and the state-room began to swim in front of Miss Briggs's eyes.

'Why don't we go in to tea now. What do you say?'

'Tea,' Miss Briggs repeated. Her voice sounded muffled and far off, as if a pillow had been placed over her mouth. She stepped down from the throne, her legs unsteady under her. The stripes of the nylon pillow-case made bars against the fading throne room.

'Yes Mrs Routledge,' she called hoarsely. 'Thank you.'

Next door she could hear Jeannette Scranton singing as she prepared for the morning ritual downstairs. It was a song she had never heard before, with a sad, almost Oriental lilt, and foreign-sounding words. Miss Briggs gritted her teeth with irritation. One of these days – no, today – she would tell Miss Scranton to pipe down with that awful sound.

'It's not what we're used to,' Cecilia Houghton said, 'but I suppose it will have to do for the time being.'

She unzipped the case of the portable and placed the machine briskly on the table – too low, she could see that already, and the chair, with its curved back and wooden seat an agony for the writer – and laid the thick manuscript down beside it before going over to the bed to unpack her clothes. Mrs Routledge had placed the novelist in Room 24, next to Miss Briggs, and on opening the cupboard that stood up against the adjoining wall she heard the sound of water running and then a soft crash, as if someone had fallen to the floor and was failing to try to get up. Mrs Houghton paused, her eyebrows rising as she stood, cocktail dress in one hand and hanger in the other, the little silver sequins on the shoulder of the gown winking at her like knowing eyes. It was early, not nine yet, and the sound was surprising for the morning, for there was something drunken and abandoned about it, the last thing she had hoped to hear in the Westringham Hotel at this hour. She had checked in (if Mrs Routledge's rough welcome could be described as checking in) as early as this in order to be able to do a full day's work undisturbed. Mrs Routledge had just announced that tea was ready downstairs. She stood by the cupboard door, unsure as to whether it was her duty to go into Room 23 and see what the matter was. Then shrugged, and slotted a fox stole on top of the cocktail dress, pushed the laden hanger on to the rod within. The trilogy would hardly be able to get under way if she became too interested in the behaviour of the characters in the hotel.

'I offer my resignation, your Majesty.'

The words came clear through the wall and Mrs Houghton flinched. Exiled royalty – not her subject matter, but irresistible all the same. She pulled a couple of cashmere sweaters out of the suitcase and laid them gently on a shelf.

'It was your Majesty's duty to continue until the end,' the voice went on. 'I never expected that you, of all people, would pull out now. If you'll forgive the language.'

Now there were sounds – creaking knees, a heavy sigh – of a person rising from an uncomfortable position on a lino floor. A tap was turned off and parts of an anatomy scrubbed. Mrs Houghton waited for the Royal answer to these accusations. But there was silence. Ill at ease, for it was bad enough having been thrown out by her sister-in-law in Knightsbridge and finding herself in this dirty, eccentric boarding house, without scenes of this kind being enacted in the adjacent room, Cecilia Houghton went over to the writing table and roused her characters in the hope they would provide some consolation.

'Just imagine, Melinda,' she said in her brightest tone. 'By tonight you and Johnny will be officially engaged! And after all you've been through – the first meeting in Czechoslovakia in '68; the bad period when you, Melinda, went in with the revolutionaries and despised Johnny for keeping his safe job; the time when you wanted to emigrate, Johnny, and Melinda had met the feminists and wouldn't go and live abroad for your sake. All over now, and you are going to settle down and live happily in the country – Dorset, I think.'

'Will I have to go off the Pill?' Melinda asked sulkily.

She had settled, as Cecilia Houghton had expected she would, on the bed beside the half-filled suitcase. The red silk dress she had been wearing last night, when she and Johnny had celebrated their engagement in a Chelsea restaurant, showed signs of fatigue but was as alluring as ever, her dark hair dishevelled now and falling on the white shoulders dotted with freckles so often described in the previous two volumes of the trilogy.

'Not yet,' her creator snapped. 'There will be problems in your marriage first. I thought you had the imagination to realize that, Melinda. As for you, Johnny, you will have to show a good deal more consideration to Melinda once you are married. Some of those bad habits – poring over your books until late in the night, the dope smoking you went in for in Volume Two – will simply have to go. Melinda may talk of independence, but hearken ye unto me, all women need attention, and plenty of it!'

Johnny had materialized over by the window and was leaning against the sill in one of his typical defiant attitudes. He avoided Mrs Houghton's bright, admonishing eye and reached in the pocket of his jeans jacket for cigarettes.

'I'm going to get you a suit,' Mrs Houghton went on, a note of cruelty in her voice. 'Once your uncle dies and leaves you the legacy, that is. You can scarcely own a small farm and go up to a show in London once a month dressed like that!'

Johnny's shoulders rose and fell in angry resignation. He glanced at Melinda, but without warmth; there seemed to be little understanding between the lovers this morning.

'It was a tiring night on the town.' Mrs Houghton finished her unpacking and smiled firmly at the young couple. At the same time she wondered if it was wise to leave them in this state, and go down to tea. Once, when she had been writing them in a first-floor suite at Bournemouth, they had disappeared while she was at lunch and she had had to go back to London to find them, two days searching Islington and the King's Cross area before finally coming across them huddled in separate corners of a disreputable pub. She had written the scene in, but reluctantly; and time and money had been wasted. It would be the last straw if they escaped the Westringham, leaving her with long blank days and the company of the other residents.

'We haven't had a meal for a long time,' Johnny said after a threatening silence. He looked more than ever today, Mrs Houghton reflected, like a mixture between Belmondo and Mick Jagger, and she wondered if she could modify his appearance slightly in the final volume. Too Sixties, she muttered under her breath as she laid out fresh paper and the little pot of white substance so essential for obliterating mistakes. But what does a Seventies man look like? Of course, age will change him. Mellow him, she corrected herself. And short hair can work wonders. Yes, a visit to the barber in the opening chapter, that's the thing.

'I thought this was meant to be realism,' Johnny said. 'You did our engagement dinner a week ago, before the trouble at Aunty Joan's. I'm starving.'

29

'I want to get out of this dress,' Melinda said. 'I stink like a polecat. Where have all my trousers gone?'

Mrs Houghton swore silently. Sometimes she wondered whether the university education she had allowed her characters hadn't been an error. Johnny had rebelliously attended lectures in English literature at London University, before dropping out and then going on to the riots at L.S.E.; Melinda had dabbled in graphic design at Hornsey. Johnny's half-baked grasp of such things as realism, imaginative writing and the use of metaphor was more irritating than Melinda's occasional pronouncements on modern art.

'You can have breakfast as soon as I've had my tea. Then off to the barber for you, Johnny. And no more trousers at the moment, Melinda. A nice coat and skirt – and perhaps a woollen dress. Now, are you both going to be good while I'm away?'

As soon as the words were out of her mouth, Mrs Houghton regretted them. Johnny clapped his hands to his long, greasy locks as if he had been promised a beheading. Melinda tore at her dress, which ripped open in front, showing the expensive new lingerie provided in her trousseau. She had never seen them look so uncooperative. And if there was one thing Cecilia Houghton dreaded it was the Block. She knew from experience that it could last for weeks, and that no amount of literary laxatives had the slightest effect on it, whether ingested in the form of the all-night reading of crime novels, or the short sharp jabs of gardening manuals. She must keep Johnny and Melinda sweet at all costs, for their relationship was of the utmost importance in the third part of the trilogy, the rôles of the other characters kept to a minimum. Where was her compassion now? How could she hope to produce well-rounded personalities if she treated them with such insensitivity? Already, Melinda looked distinctly two-dimensional in her torn dress on the bed. Johnny resembled a cardboard cutout in his menacing attitude against the window.

'Forgive me!' Mrs Houghton went over to both and stroked them lovingly. Johnny, who had shown an evil streak at the Encounter Group therapy session to which Mrs Houghton had taken him in the first volume, shook her off roughly. Melinda

30

gave a better response, filling out under Mrs Houghton's gentle fingers. An idea flitted into the writer's mind.

'You know I want you to say what's going to happen! I want you to take over completely, and many times you have, my dears, only needing to be pulled in from time to time for the sake of the structure. Suppose we all sit down when I've had my tea –'

'And we've had our breakfast,' Melinda put in, tears in her large eyes.

'Yes, yes. And then we can decide together what comes next. In the meantime, I'd like you to do a little detective work for me. There's most definitely something odd happening in this hotel. And you are uniquely well placed to find out what it is.'

'Something odd?' Johnny's eyes brightened for a moment. Then he glared again. 'Your idea of something odd is a man forgetting to send flowers on his wife's anniversary, Mrs H. Sorry but I'm just not into sniffing round the marital rows in this dump.'

'Not at all! There's exiled royalty undergoing torture in the next room, Johnny. I heard it before you woke up. Now why don't you slip in there in a minute and then report back later?'

Some of the old life seemed to be returning to the characters, because both Melinda and Johnny burst out laughing and Johnny threw his cigarette end out of the window with his usual aplomb.

'And I don't have to go to the barber?' he said after a pause.

'Not if you don't want to,' Mrs Houghton lied. 'No, some king or queen of a forgotten country is confined in there. You know my curiosity, Johnny. Melinda, will you?'

The idea was working well. Johnny and Melinda went to the door and Mrs Houghton showed them into the passage, then headed for the stairs and the welcome cup of tea.

'You really shouldn't let your imagination run away with you like this, Mrs H.,' Johnny shouted down at her. She heard the door of Room 23 open and then close again, and smiled with satisfaction. He had really sounded quite affectionate this time.

'Cridge!'

Mrs Routledge peered down the dark stairs that led from the dining-room of the Westringham Hotel to the black basement where her servant lived. She was used to the smell, which was like stagnant water at the bottom of an enamel pitcher and a horrible sweetness thrown in, the effect of Cridge's tobacco on the stale, damp air, but this morning it was particularly sickening. Cridge had a habit of defecating in a selection of antique jars and vases stored there and forgotten by a former resident, and on Thursdays he would come up, go through the dining-room with them and empty them in the Gentleman's Cloaks behind the reception desk in the front hall. Today was Wednesday. Mrs Routledge wobbled over the top step, her nostrils drawn together and her eyes searching the gloomy air for the man.

'Cridge, you'll serve the tea, please. Come up at once.'

The top of Cridge's head appeared a few steps below Mrs Routledge. It was yellow and striped with grey hair, like a badger. His eyes, of the same colour but with an admixture of red from the long hours spent under the Westringham, looked up at her without expression. Mrs Routledge sighed with disgust. Cridge had been with her only two years, but his abject stance and the atmosphere of hopeless servility which emanated from his threadbare naval jacket and worn slippers often led her to think that he had obeyed her every command since childhood. Sometimes, on Thursday evenings when the air from the basement was cleaner and Mrs Routledge permitted one of the residents to treat her to a sherry from the bar, she boasted that Cridge had been the butler in her father's mansion in Worcestershire. 'He used to give me piggy-backs. Didn't you, Cridge? And of course' – here she would give a little smile, modest and self-deprecating, showing that even the upper classes could suffer deprivation in their up-bringing – 'I saw more of Cridge than I did of my own parents. We children were brought up by the staff, you know. Dressed in our finery and brought down to tea in the drawing-room. That kind of thing!' Now, as the wretched figure lurched past her into the little room with its arrangement of five tables, plastic ferns and thick teacups upside down on the sideboard, she repressed her loathing and attempted a tone both brisk and friendly. This was for the benefit of Mrs Houghton, who had booked in early this morning and spoken of grand relations who had had to move temporarily out of their house in Knightsbridge while it was undergoing redecoration.

'And not so many lumps of sugar in the bowl, Cridge,' she hissed. 'Two each is quite sufficient.'

Steps sounded on the flight of stairs that led to the first-floor bedrooms and Mrs Routledge gave Cridge a sharp nudge in the ribs.

'Yes, Miss Amanda,' said Cridge, in response to this particular blow. He shuffled over to the sideboard, turned the cups to a receptive position, and with an unsteady hand poured the tea into them. For a moment his lingering subterranean smell was obliterated by P G Tips. Mrs Houghton, for indeed it was she, swept into the dining-room and then stopped dead. Mrs Routledge was accustomed to this first reaction from her guests and went towards her with a wide smile.

'This is your table, Mrs Houghton. Near the door, of course.'

'Thank you.' Mrs Houghton took a handkerchief from the crocodile handbag in her hand and covered her nose, then made a pretence of blowing it. She sat down heavily on the little gilt chair. Mrs Routledge saw that the handkerchief was of poor quality. She then wondered about the crocodile. A scarcely visible film of hardness passed over her features.

'A very pleasant part of London,' Mrs Houghton remarked. 'It does one good to change one's ambience from time to time, don't you agree?'

Mrs Routledge still stood staring at her suspiciously, and the novelist hoisted her bag on to the table, knocking over the plastic fern as she did so.

'I'm so sorry.' She readjusted the tiny, waterless container and drew from her bag this time a gold initialled cigarette case and matching lighter. The cigarette once in her mouth, she pressed what appeared to be a sapphire button on the lighter, and flame sprang reassuringly upwards. Mrs Routledge's features softened.

'There seem to be problems in the room next to mine,' Mrs Houghton said, taking advantage of this. 'Not that I don't have the greatest sympathy for the poor things. An eastern-European country, I suppose.'

'What do you mean?' Mrs Routledge was suspicious again, but with different cause. She had had people suffering from mental illness trying to hide out in the Westringham before. And there had been sounds of speech from Mrs Houghton's room, never a good sign.

'I mean, of course, some exiled monarch or other . . .' Mrs Houghton's voice tailed off. 'I didn't feel, somehow, it was one of ours. If you know what I mean, Mrs Routledge.'

At this juncture Mr Poynter manifested himself on the stairs and came into the dining-room. At the same time, Cridge put a cup of tea down in front of Mrs Houghton. He had mixed in condensed milk and two lumps of greyish sugar stood on the saucer.

'Good heavens,' Mrs Houghton said. She was gazing at Cridge. And the crocodile bag slipped from her lap to the floor, where it lay on its side, handles a ready trap for Mr Poynter's feet. Mr Poynter, however, avoided this.

'Deposed kings,' he said ruminatively. 'I thought I had them all by now, I must say.' He looked sternly down at Mrs Houghton. 'Poynter. Lieutenant-Colonel Arthur Poynter. And may I have the pleasure . . . ?'

'This is too extraordinary.' Mrs Houghton smiled at Cridge, who was backing away now and making for the tin of condensed milk, dolloping in the spoonfuls in a near panic. 'He was in Volume One of the trilogy, you know, Mrs Routledge! A dear little hotel in Norfolk, when Johnny and Melinda had just come back from Czechoslovakia and wanted to get away from it all. Cridge – you were the boatman. Oh, that bitterly cold weather.

And your blue-veined hands! Melinda was so sorry for you, but then she saw you had made no attempt to join the struggle against capitalism and neo-imperialism. Yes, Johnny had to persuade her not to give you a good talking to at the end of that long day in the creek.'

'What's all this?' Mr Poynter strode over to his table and exchanged glances with Mrs Routledge on the way. Cridge, who might not have heard a word of his former creator's speech, went over to him with an uneven gait and slopped down the tea.

'My table's been moved, Mrs Routledge.' Poynter stood dumbfounded at the top of the basement steps, where indeed, in her effort to please Mrs Houghton, Mrs Routledge had placed him. The sweet, acrid stench reached his nostrils. He thumped the table and his fern – dusted that morning, he could see – quivered in response. 'I demand an explanation,' he went on, in the face of Mrs Routledge's silence, and Cridge, limping back to the sideboard. Mr Poynter had once told Cridge that he reminded him of his wounded batman and the limp was now a matter of course when he was being served.

'Have I taken your table? I'm so terribly sorry, I had no idea.'

'The rules of the house,' Mrs Routledge snapped at her two guests. 'We had a spring clean, Colonel. And we all need some variety sometimes. So there we are, I'm afraid.'

Miss Briggs came down the stairs, followed closely by Miss Scranton. They, too, stopped at the threshold of the dining-room, but as both were acquainted with Cridge's basement odours it was the double shock of seeing a new resident at the best table by the door and a look of implacable hatred on the face of Mr Poynter which brought them to a halt. Mrs Routledge bustled at them and ushered them to their respective seats. This was even more surprising. Miss Scranton sipped at her scalding tea and Miss Briggs, still stunned by the behaviour of her Queen the night before, stared vacantly around her.

'This is Miss Scranton. Miss Scranton, Mrs Houghton. And this is Miss Briggs.' Mrs Routledge escaped to the reception desk in the hall after effecting the introductions. She sat on the high leather stool behind the desk and pretended to sort through mail, but she felt shaken and was unable to bring herself to look up and meet the eye of either Mr Poynter or Cridge. Something would have to be done about this woman with her gold cigarette case and illusions of royalty in the hotel; her impossible recognition of Cridge. Mrs Routledge wished her husband was alive, then remembered how she had dealt with these problems before. A call to Mr Rathbone's office. Get through and speak to Mr Rathbone personally, if necessary. As the chairman of the company which owned the property, he would be as anxious as she to evict undesirable persons – potential arsonists, possibly – from the premises. She slid her hand into a cubbyhole under the desk and pulled out her address book, running a ringed finger down to the letter R. Yes, there he was. But she must wait until tea was over and the residents safely back in their rooms before making the call.

Slight murmurs of conversation drifted in from the dining-room. Mr Poynter appeared to have discovered that he knew some relations of Mrs Houghton's. Miss Briggs also claimed she had met them at a recent garden party. Cridge was refilling the cups and handing bread and butter as if nothing had happened. Mrs Routledge wavered. Anything to avoid trouble; and if Mrs Houghton's family was important enough to compensate Mr Poynter for the terrible new position of his table it would perhaps be better to leave well alone and see how things went for another day or two. Mrs Routledge risked a searching glance into the room where her guests were sitting. Miss Briggs was hushed and effusive. Cridge limped frequently to Poynter, bringing with him, she saw, an unallowable quantity of sugar. Mrs Houghton's bag was now upright and she smiled and chatted and lit up cigarettes by pressing the little sapphire button.

Only Miss Scranton was silent. Mrs Routledge gazed at her. Her eyes grew wide, then closed in horror and disbelief. Miss Scranton's legs and feet were bare and thickly coated with what appeared to be sand. It was too much. Mrs Routledge wondered whether Mrs Houghton had noticed and, if so, whether she would lodge a complaint to the company over the standards of hygiene in the hotel. She imagined an inspection of the basement, and shuddered. Miss Scranton finished her tea and pulled a couple of exercise books from her satchel. She leant back in her chair, her sandy legs sticking out on the carpet. But the others seemed to have seen nothing as yet. Mrs Routledge felt a headache coming on. She slipped out unobtrusively from behind the desk and went up to her second-floor bedroom to take an aspirin and lie down.

When tea was over Mr Poynter went up to his room trembling with excitement. He sat down on the edge of his bed and put his head in his hands, staring out through bony fingers at the lumps under the lino, and the greasy film of curtain against the closed window, and the hanging bulb in the little parchment shade that trembled every time Mrs Routledge got in or out of her divan on the floor above. He was sure he had seen Cecilia Houghton somewhere before – in his City, of course – at one of the evenings given by the cultural attaché perhaps, or in the salon of Lady Kitty Carson, a literary hostess slightly inaccurately imagined by Mr Poynter but able to function nevertheless in a small antique-crammed house near the moving quarter. Yes; it must have been there: he saw Lady Kitty in her Retour d'Egypte chair, the literary lions of the megalopolis gathered at her feet, the epigrams coming out sharp and smooth as the cheese biscuits were handed and good wine was poured. He saw Cecilia Houghton, dignified and aloof, amused at the spectacle Lady Kitty made of herself on these occasions, and even imagined himself exchanging glances with her. Really Creative People like Mrs Houghton (and himself, he had to add this) always found these hostess figures a bit of a joke. But they were necessary: even the staidest novelist or historian needed to relax and show off sometimes; once or twice a year a cruel parody of Lady Kitty appeared in one of their books and was then serialized in the City Sundays. Cecilia had probably gone there, as he did, to show she felt no spite towards her fellow workers.

What a stroke of luck to find her suddenly at the Westringham, though! Mr Poynter smiled out through his fingers, and caught sight of his watch on his hairless wrist as he did so. He took off his clothes and pulled on a pair of musty red and white striped pyjamas. He padded to the window and wrestled with the inadequate curtain. He climbed into bed. There was ample time before lunch to meet Cecilia Houghton again. To show her who he really was. Not, of course, that she hadn't known at once in the dining-room, but in the presence of others one must be discreet . . . He closed his eyes and a blissful sigh escaped him before he slept. The niece of Field-Marshal Sir Eddie Houghton . . . he remembered her coming-out ball in the *Tatler*. And such a brilliant novelist too! She had informed him over Cridge's revolting tea that her work was taught all over the world. He wasn't surprised. Today she would be entertained at HQ; a banquet with roses and champagne. He tried to decide whether she would like to meet his wife – or was there, possibly, a romance brooding between them? A meeting of equals? A faint snore issued from Mr Poynter as he approached the four-walled city of his dreams.

Today, although at least an hour and a half had passed since Poynter had been woken and gone downstairs, the sun seemed to show no change of position in the sky. The City was still in the early morning stage, the sprinklers refreshing the bright green turf, the workers hurrying to their production lines within the thick walls of the town as if he had only just completed the morning parade and was not yet even on his way to visit his wife. Mr Poynter frowned. Sometimes this happened – like a record with the needle stuck in a groove the same dream would repeat itself – and he prayed, as he strode from the portals of HQ and saw the white Rolls waiting there, that he would not have to undergo the tiresome experience this morning. Of all mornings! Somewhere in the City Mrs Houghton awaited him – he was sure of that – in the Central Park probably, under the trimmed pink apple blossom, or in the National Portrait Gallery, where her uncle's portrait (almost as many versions of the Field-Marshal as of Mr Poynter himself) hung in the dark rooms. Or at Lady Kitty's, at a literary luncheon: they would smile at each other at the pretensions of the woman and then go strolling hand in hand in the portion of the park reserved for upper ranks. Mr Poynter's frown turned to an audible curse when he saw his chauffeur come out to admit him to his car.

'Where are we going, my man?'

'To the Poynter Residence, Sir.'

Poynter's shoulders sagged. When the dream got into one of its self-repeating states urgent measures were called for. The people became discontented and sometimes actually rebellious at the total sameness of things, booing their leader's speeches on reforms and progress from the balcony. The lack of darkness (or light, if this catastrophic event occurred at night) threw out their digestions and there were complaints of eyeache and headache. Barricades could only too easily go up in the ghetto, if the streets happened to be narrow at the time, and home-made weapons were directed at the troops. Usually, there was a short insurrection and much bloodshed. Mrs Poynter hated violence; so, Poynter remembered from his conversation at morning tea, did Cecilia; and a bad impression of the City would be registered on the novelist. Further, and here Mr Poynter stopped cursing and groaned aloud, it was his daughter's ball tonight. Nothing appeared more squalid, in a peaceful, well-run State, than the sight of the Top Rank cavorting in a surround of Security Guards. To cancel the ball was out of the question, even if it had to take place in the light from the early morning sun. It would be an admission of weakness, of fear at the consequences. He thought of giving orders to leave the candles in the great chandeliers unlit, but realized he was already admitting defeat to himself. Something must be done; and quickly and subtly now, before the populace looked up to see the sun at its zenith and understood the truth. He took the chauffeur's arm and led him a few steps to the side of the car, out of earshot of the sentry.

'I don't want to go my wife's house at the moment. Do you hear me? I want to be taken to the park, and then on to Lady Kitty Carson's. Possibly the Portrait Gallery. And be sharp about it, will you?'

Poynter went to the car and opened the door himself. He was convinced now that only Cecilia Houghton could solve this problem for him. With her ingenuity and love of moderation . . . he swung himself half into the deeply padded seats and then stopped, his body in the position of a sitting man but only air under him and the surprised face of the chauffeur looking down into his eyes.

'I'm sorry sir. But those were Orders. It's your wife's Residence

we're going to.' The chauffeur climbed into the dr'
instantly Poynter was released from his discom
himself sitting in the back, the car purring softly at a
ten miles an hour towards the smart district. He gritted hi
in rage.

'Didn't you hear me?'

'You remember what happened last time, Sir.'

So the man knew! Perhaps it was later than Poynter thought –
after noon and trouble already brewing in the ghetto. Perhaps he
even knew of the terrible time when Mr Poynter had found himself stuck there, endlessly repeating the Victorian fetishistic
fantasies which had seemed so entertaining at the beginning of the
evening – it had been touch and go then, with Poynter's First-in-
Command having to quell the insurrection while the leader went
on hands and knees, again and again, to kiss the dainty laced boots
and frilled camiknickers of the exhausted girls, as to whether the
City would fall to the revolutionaries or control would be regained. Mr Poynter shuddered. Rumours travelled fast in the
City, however hard he tried to repress them.

'Very well then.' He spoke in a dignified tone. It was true that
the re-enacting of the preceding sequence had never worked
before, and things had always remained stubbornly stuck until
the use of violence was the only means, but it was worth trying.
Cecilia would almost certainly approve of his efforts, he reflected
as the car carried him inexorably past the neat front gardens and
down Rainbow Avenue to his wife's house. He would have done
what he could. But the thought of his wife – and the unpleasant
sandy marks on the lawn and the drawing-room carpet, too –
filled him with displeasure and disgust. The only hope was to try
and speed the thing up – or it would be lunchtime and still no
glimpse of Mrs Houghton at all. He raced through the early
morning's events in his head, deciding to cut out Mrs Poynter's
expressions of astonishment and grief.

The first part of the scene did indeed seem to go more quickly.
Poynter went through the sprinklers at double speed, so that he
emerged at the front steps of his house only slightly damp; and
this time, keeping his eyes carefully averted from the lawn, he
managed to miss out the muddy trail which had proved so un-

41

leasant a part of the early morning dream. He went through the blue hall at a gallop, and arrived in the heavenly drawing-room, hand held out in front of him in the effort to stall the breakdown and recovery sequence on the part of his wife. His heart was racing; but he felt it was only a matter of seconds before he was back in the car again, the sun mounting the sky to the meridian, and Cecilia captured. What met his gaze, instead of bringing him to the standstill so common in his City (he wondered sometimes if these stoppages were due to a missed heartbeat while sleeping) led him to increase his velocity – and it was only by flinging himself at the trunk of the ancient oak on the sward beyond the french windows that he was able to come to a halt at all. The bump against the knotted oak shook him considerably, and he stood dazed for a moment, spreadeagled on the solid expanse of his famous heritage.

The drawing-room, through which Mr Poynter had shot at a speed that must surely have rendered him invisible to its occupants, was littered with the forms of huge, sated and sleeping women. Their sandy buttocks made an undulating mound of pale flesh. Their hair, stiff with salt and mud, lay like twisted rope on the pile carpets, their great arms were intertwined and their brown eyes were lazily open, lying like puddles of forgotten water when the tide has left the beach. In his race over their recumbent bodies, Poynter had seen his wife – brown-eyed too now, and as naked as the rest – and, to his particular horror, what appeared to be Miss Scranton, small and scrawny but bearing nevertheless the same marks of recent and passionate lovemaking. Piles of soldiers' uniforms stood up against the walls of the drawing-room, obscuring Old Masters and vases of herbaceous flowers on the gilt and marble consoles. The uniforms belonged to the Forty-Five, his most reliable battalion. Poynter closed his eyes and felt in the pocket of his breeches for a handkerchief.

'My dear Lieutenant-Colonel.' A soft, already beloved voice sounded in his ear but he kept his eyes closed, not believing.

'I came out here to find you. As I so much looked forward to meeting your wife. There seems to have been some kind of mishap. May I give you the advice my uncle the Field-Marshal once gave me?'

Poynter opened his eyes and despite the tragedy in his Residence found himself smiling in welcome. Cecilia Houghton stood before him. She was wearing a crushed-pink taffeta dress and matching hat, and from her pale wrists a pair of elbow-length, white kid gloves dangled elegantly.

'Cecilia! I don't know what to say . . .'

'We must repair the damage, Arthur. These . . . these Amazons have raped and looted. I took the liberty of calling HQ and ordering the Special Police to come up here forthwith. As my uncle said, it's never as late as you think.'

Poynter rubbed at his eyes and wished they were closed again. He wondered if the famous lady writer was aware that his wife was amongst the pile of hideous flesh. And had she recognized Miss Scranton, from the short meeting at early morning tea? She would be bound to leave the Westringham now, to relegate their meetings to the regions of sleep alone.

'I won't abandon you,' Mrs Houghton said, as if capable of reading his thoughts. 'I'm here to help you, Arthur. And look, here are your men. All will be well in no time.'

As Cecilia spoke, Poynter's Special Police Force swept into the Residence and the familiar, acrid smell of tear gas filled the pleasant morning air. Poynter gave a sigh of relief and glanced up at the sky. If only the sun would move. He imagined himself dancing gratefully with Mrs Houghton tonight at the ball, while his wife recuperated from her shock in the military hospital. But the sun was still, idiotically, at a pristine, matutinal slant. He reached out and took hold of his saviour's hand.

'Cecilia, I can't thank you enough . . .'

Coughing and choking, the giantesses were led, docile, through the drawing-room and down the hall to the waiting police vans. Poynter watched them go, glancing away at the sight of his wife's naked posterior and the pathetic, slouching gait adopted by Miss Scranton. Servants came in and tidied the room, spraying the pine-flavoured essence in the gas-laden air and restoring the deep sofas and little occasional tables to their accustomed positions. Mrs Houghton returned the pressure of Mr Poynter's hand.

'I think it's safe to go in there and order a little snack, don't you, Arthur? And don't worry about . . . well about the day not progressing as it should. I'm sure we'll be able to get that under control too. Come along, you must be hungry. How about anchovies on toast? Or something a mite more substantial?'

Concealing his tears of gratitude, Poynter followed Mrs Houghton into the house. For a moment the idea of divorcing his wife and marrying Mrs Houghton flashed through his mind, then he dismissed it. In Mr Poynter's City, divorce was strictly forbidden and it was for him to set a good example to the mob.

Jeannette Scranton climbed back into bed eagerly after the unnecessary tea break and closed her eyes. Memories of the irritating woman who seemed to have completely taken over the dining-room with her crocodile handbag and gold cigarette case, and the strange atmosphere her presence had engendered – Mrs Routledge both excited and suspicious, Mr Poynter courtly, and old Cridge verging on a state of catatonia – soon faded from the teacher's mind. She was on the great plain and the men were visible now, the scarlet tunics of their uniforms glowing in the torchlight and the horses whinnying as they came at full gallop to the women's leafy tents. Miss Scranton felt calm, more prepared than she had imagined possible for the soon to be consummated ritual.

The women rose to their feet and stood tall and silent before their partners. Miss Scranton followed suit. The men dismounted. Miss Scranton's hand was grasped. She was lifted on to a horse. The saddle was warm and inviting beneath her naked flanks. She smiled, and a burst of song escaped from her lips. The moon was full. The air smelled of thyme and honey. A soldier leapt on to the saddle in front of her and the horse began to move forward. Miss Scranton's breasts quivered and bounced. She had never felt so happy. She looked back at the other women and their escorts, her hand raised in a gracious wave. Then, as the steed broke into a canter under her, she saw that all was not well at the encampment and that it was too late to go back.

The women were wailing and gnashing their teeth and putting up resistance to the men. They were outnumbered and the men were lashing them to the backs of the horses by their long, sandy hair. One of the women, the largest and most terrifying in aspect, was attacking her captors with a flaming torch; the little wooden constructions in which they had waited for their mates caught fire; as Miss Scranton receded powerless from the scene, she saw the giantess fighting there, smoke billowing from her matted tresses and flames licking at her rough, wide legs. The men shouted in triumph and spurred their mounts up into the hills behind Miss Scranton. Each carried its heavy, protesting load. Soon the other soldiers were level with her and she could see the gagged faces of the women, their eyes giving out for the first time hatred and hostility and fear.

Miss Scranton's heart sank. It seemed she had got everything wrong again. If she had stopped to think – and this was a complaint she often heard in the staff-room – she would have realized that these uniformed soldiers were hardly the gentle, goddess-worshipping men met once yearly by the Amazons for the propagation of the female species. The aggressors looked, if anything, dressed for a musical comedy in the 1890s. They had small neat moustaches, their tunics were gold-buttoned, and a toy sword poked from a scabbard at their sides. Their eyes were a bright Prussian blue. Miss Scranton had a horrible feeling that she was being taken back at full speed to the world of her childhood years, when men such as these were her brothers' heroes, and stupefying afternoons were spent outside Buckingham Palace watching the changing of the guard. All her desire and happiness vanished. At the same time she was afraid: of the reprisals of the women at her joyous welcome – for she had betrayed them, there was no doubt about that; she had put up no fight at all – and of the forthcoming embraces in the arms of these brutal military men. Miss Scranton's dream had turned to a nightmare. Every soldier seemed to possess the unbearable, proud features of her father; even the sound of their shouting voices was a forcible reminder of why she had never, however great her mother's disappointment, gone to the altar as a bride.

The convoy reached the top of the hill and Miss Scranton was able to look down at the landscape below. The Ancient Greek mountains to which she had become accustomed since her dreams in the Westringham began had disappeared, and in their place was a neat English landscape. Downs bearing the marks of Roman invasion, Saxon tillage, trammelled with hedgerows and narrow lanes and sewn into a patchwork of multicoloured fields, stretched out before her. The moon, too, was small, and hung like the electric light bulb in her bedroom over the spire of a market-town cathedral. Sluggish streams made dark shadows in the shallow valleys. A moan from the gagged women went up as they too saw the country of Miss Scranton's birth. The horses began to walk slowly down through stubble, the saddles creaking and slipping as they went. For a moment Miss Scranton wondered if she would be able to help them in their escape by identifying the country they were in. There was something familiar about it – could it be Hampshire? – but the absence of highrise buildings and urban sprawl made this seem unlikely. It was as if England, like the soldiers, had been arrested at some point near the beginning of the century. The beach, the long hut, seemed irrecoverably far away. Miss Scranton would never be able to get herself or her sisters out of this. She jogged on behind her captor, hands folded for safety's sake around the thin red felt of his tunic.

When two streams had been forded and several valleys left behind, the soldiers and the women arrived at a great gate set in a thick wall of white marble. The gate swung open and the convoy went in. Miss Scranton, exhausted as she was, saw that it was early morning here: the sun was climbing the sky, jets of water splashed on the façades of the spotless houses, birdsong filled the air. Despite her fear of the other women and her dread of the rape which must surely take place soon, her spirits lifted a little. Miss Scranton loved cleanliness. Wonderful though her life had been on the timeless pre-Helladic beach, the sight of the well-proportioned streets, each house with its soil pipe and flowery window box, was somehow comforting and reassuring. She looked down at her sand-encrusted legs and promised herself a bubble bath as soon as the fiesta was over – flannels, loofahs and nail brushes, all forgotten objects of her previous life sprang into her mind. It was clear from the continued muffled protests of her sisters that they felt no such anticipation. However – and here Miss Scranton felt hopeful again – a happy compromise might be reached. It was possible that the rulers of this town, whomsoever they might be, would allot to the women a pleasant hygienic quarter where there would be plenty of baths, peace, and good food brought to them at regular intervals. Miss Scranton realized it might take a long time to persuade the Amazons of the advantages of harem conditions, but she hoped that in the end they would come to their senses. Otherwise there would be mass slaughter. Going at a stately trot through the newly paved streets, she tried to communicate this message to them with the eye language of the past. But they looked back at her with stubbornness and incomprehension. Their eyes, even, appeared to have lost the rich fire that had burned in them on the beach.

The horses went over Mr Poynter's lawn and Miss Scranton shuddered at the hoof marks on the rich turf. She saw a beautiful woman in a blue gown and wimple standing by the french windows of what was without doubt the most important house in the city. She waved and dismounted, waiting impatiently on the sward while the soldiers untied the women. Then, as the great, sulking captives were pushed over the grass and in through the open windows, she skipped to the head of the line and smiled up at the beautiful woman. The beautiful woman smiled back, and when Miss Scranton had come right up to her asked for assistance in disrobing herself of her stiff and richly embroidered gown so that she, too, could be naked. Miss Scranton felt reassured at this. Her chafed hands, coarse with sand and sea water, fumbled with the tiny, silken hooks and eyes. When it was time to lie down and wait on the deep fitted carpet, she chose to lie beside the beautiful woman, to suffer the forthcoming indignity with the same degree of stoicism exhibited by the mistress of the house.

The soldiers tied the Amazons down, securing thick wrists and ankles to drawing-room tables and chairs. The floor of the room undulated with their breasts, like a desert sea; their nipples, which looked like dried flowers, made splashes of dull brown red. They seemed resigned now, and accepting of their fate. Miss Scranton saw that they had closed their eyes. She glanced at the beautiful woman, saw the perfect blue of her orbs cloud with brown, as if a muddy spring was welling up in them. Then the eyelids went down. Miss Scranton followed suit, and waited.

The rape seemed to take a long time. Miss Scranton thought of her multiplication tables as the sharp thrusting went on, and then of the essays on The Best Day of the Holidays which were still uncorrected in her satchel bag. She remembered she had left the satchel bag behind on the plain, in her haste to greet the captors, and groaned aloud. All round her the Amazons were groaning, the rope on their wrists and ankles snapping as their powerful bodies heaved and writhed. Their coarse hair rubbed loudly on the carpet. Only the beautiful woman was silent, and Miss Scranton promised herself not to make another sound, even though the loss of the satchel would probably cost her her job, and the pain from the organs of the soldiers was reaching an unbearable level. The beautiful woman reminded her of the National Gallery postcard she had once worshipped, when she had been the age of her poor, neglected pupils – the Virgin Mary – by Leonardo? – by Fra Angelico? – her mind began to wander, and as the moaning and screeching rose to a crescendo, and flesh slapped against flesh with the horrible, final sound of a dead catch from the sea going down on marble slabs, Miss Scranton at last lost consciousness. When she opened her eyes again, the soldiers had gone. She sat up tentatively, and examined the scene.

The Amazons and the beautiful woman were sleeping peacefully, and a faint, snoring rumble filled the room, taking Miss Scranton back in her ever-eager memory to the drone of bees at her aunt's house, the sweet william and peonies that grew in abundance there, the time when she had thought herself in love with the vicar's son. The soldiers' uniforms, she saw, were piled against the walls, and she wondered if this was a deliberate gesture, to indicate to their General that they would no longer fight wars for him. Miss Scranton felt surprisingly well and refreshed. Her mind was clear. The leaving behind of the satchel no longer seemed such a tragedy, as she had no intention of returning to the school. This City was the perfect place to be. She tried to imagine the delightful quarters she would be given – as a special friend of the mistress of the house she would certainly have apartments of her own – and came to the conclusion that it was time to wake the Amazons. They must all take their baths now, and acclimatize themselves to the new life. It was then that she saw Mr Poynter pass through the room, at a speed which led her to rub her eyes and tell herself she must be imagining things. He was there – and then he was gone – and Mr Poynter of all people! A brownish blush spread over Miss Scranton's body, and she reached for the lacy tablecloth, which hung draped over the nearest occasional table, in an attempt to cover herself. Too late, of course – but suppose he had come to rest out in the garden, suppose he had seen her – Miss Scranton thought of lunch at the Westringham, and Mr Poynter's eyes over the plastic fern, and gazed anxiously out at the lawn for a glimpse of him.

Mr Poynter was there; and, worse still, he was talking animatedly to the dreadful lady who had arrived at the hotel this morning. Mrs Houghton was wearing a silk dress and hat, and there was something about the style of her clothes that made Miss Scranton feel more naked than ever. After they had smiled at each other inanely for a few minutes, Mr Poynter and Mrs Houghton looked up in the direction of the french windows and relief appeared on their faces. Miss Scranton smelled something sweet and strong and bitter at the same time and began to gasp for breath. She tried to push her way over to the windows – she hardly cared now if they saw her in the nude, she was suffocating, she must be got out of this immediately – but strong dark blue arms grabbed her from behind. There was an outburst of screaming and coughing in the room, and then silence. Miss Scranton had a handkerchief placed over her mouth by the policemen. With the others, she was led out to the vans. But the feeling of suffocation persisted; and when she woke, to the familiar Wednesday lunch smell of shepherd's pie and carrots, she rose from her pillow wheezing and gulping at the air. She wondered, as she prepared herself shakily for the dining-room, whether she was having a recurrence of those fits of childhood asthma.

Mrs Routledge lay in her bed and thought about the future, which, these days, only seemed capable of presenting itself as a revamped and frequently misty version of the past. She knew that Mr Rathbone and his Group of Companies, whatever they were, were considering the possibility of pulling down the West-ringham and the accompanying houses in the terrace; that a state of general anaesthesia, so to speak, was being administered to the occupants – deafness to requests for repairs and maintenance, blindness to the carious condition of the façades, the rotting beams and sagging floorboards within, numb, puzzled smiles in response to the occasional angry demonstration – before, all of a sudden, the buildings were extracted and a row of dusty stumps remained, ready for redevelopment; but she could see no further than herself in some other Westringham, kindly moved there by Mr Rathbone and everything much the same as before if not a good deal better. In fact, when the move came, she saw herself stepping out of the house twenty years younger. Suitors would present themselves in the new Westringham and she would probably remarry. Seeing the future like this, Mrs Routledge had everything to look forward to and nothing to dread. The last couple of decades, since Mr Routledge's death and the necessity to turn a delightful home into what she could privately admit to herself was a low-standard boarding house, had been nothing but a silly mistake. Mr Rathbone, who had assumed husbandly and godly proportions in Mrs Routledge's mind, would make her young and comfortable elsewhere. Sometimes she wondered if the time was ripe yet to meet him. But she was never feeling quite up to it. If she went to his office in the clothes she wore at the Westringham she would look eccentric and his secretaries might laugh. If he came to her, there was the problem of the basement, and the peculiarity of the residents, who seemed perfectly ordinary on admission but soon started to sleep obsessively, as if the doomed atmosphere of the area had turned the modest hotel into some latter-day temple to Aesculapius. He would be bound to find the place unattractive. Mrs Routledge wished she could set out, as Cecilia Houghton had this morning, on a round of shops and boutiques, fit herself up for the meeting with Mr Rathbone. Mrs Houghton had left for Harrods, complaining loudly that this was a bad part of London for taxis. It was years since Mrs Routledge had left the crumbling crescents and fly-blown grocery stores that surrounded the Westringham and crept under the Westway; so long that she could hardly remember what a respectable district looked like, permeated as she was with the experience of living in something that was unnecessary and threatened, like a rumbling appendix. She imagined the streets were clean, and the buildings of uniform height. Sometimes she dreamed she was in a wonderful place like that, but Mr Poynter always appeared in the dream and she took care to wake herself up. Mrs Routledge had no fondness for Mr Poynter, for all his pretensions. When she found herself in a neat residential quarter, and saw him coming towards her through a well-tended garden abloom with fuchsias (dressed in some ridiculous outfit, usually), she asked loudly if this was where Mr Rathbone lived and was instantly woken by his infuriated response. At tea, on the mornings after these dreams, neither she nor Mr Poynter made any reference to the unintended meeting. In the Westringham, at least, it was Mrs Routledge who was in control and not the other way around. She had feared for some time that Mr Poynter, as the only male resident, would try and take charge of the place and relegate her to the status of some kind of elevated housekeeper. He had appeared at tea a few months ago in a scarlet military tunic with gold tassels and had shouted at Cridge. She had made it perfectly clear that this would not happen again. But sometimes she was afraid to drop off to sleep, in case of seeing him in that beautiful place. If only Mr Rathbone would appear there once, and show him who really belonged where! It was time she pulled herself together and got Mr Rathbone on her side.

With eyes half closed in pleasant reverie, Mrs Routledge

imagined herself in the cocktail-dress department of Harrods, side by side with Cecilia Houghton but infinitely more splendidly attired. She smiled to herself as she lay on the pink bed, the brownish half-moons left by her own greasy head and that of the late Mr Routledge (paler than hers, but still a vivid reminder of their marriage) hanging above her on the padded chintz bedhead like signs from some long-forgotten corporeal zodiac. The sun came in through the window and lit up the frilly lampshades and the silk curtains, hemmed with rows of greying white bobbles. A large fly, woken by the spring heat, droned about the room and settled on her foot. Mrs Routledge waggled her toes and thought of Miss Scranton and the sand at tea that morning. The smile slowly faded from her face. Where could Miss Scranton have found a sand-pit? Had she regressed to childhood, a possibility she had read about in one of the new psychology magazines she leafed through in the newsagent on the corner? Or was this part of what Miss Scranton called a 'project' at the school where she taught? Whatever it was, it didn't look good. Mrs Routledge remembered that even if she did buy herself a new dress and invite Mr Rathbone to the Westringham, there was the risk of Miss Scranton's sandy feet spoiling everything. She sighed; and made a mental note to invite the residents for sherry in the dining-room tomorrow evening, Thursday, when the basement had been cleaned out. It was the only way, as she often explained to them, of airing problems and grievances, even if it did too frequently become a mutual criticism session. She would tell Miss Scranton then that shoes and stockings were *de rigueur* in the hotel, and she would do it before Mrs Houghton came down for the drink. Thinking about these difficulties made Mrs Routledge's eyes open again and she sat up, looking accusingly round the familiar room as if her clients were already there and awaiting her expressions of disapproval. She felt restless and dissatisfied. Perhaps she would go to Miss Scranton now and get it over – call on all the guests in turn and inform them that a very important person was invited for sherry tomorrow. That their future depended on the way they conducted themselves on that occasion. The more she considered the idea, the better it seemed to Mrs Routledge. Her hand went out to the address book on the bedside table, and then paused. It would be more sensible to ascertain the condition of the residents of the Westringham before giving the invitation. When one was normal, another could be decidedly odd. She pulled on her mules, and hoisted her heavy body off the side of the bed.

A clear voice was speaking on the landing of the floor below. Mrs Routledge frowned; the voice was instantly recognizable but she couldn't quite place it; she went to the door and shuffled over to the banister to look down. She recalled, as she peered through the gloom, that Mrs Houghton had complained of there being someone in Miss Briggs's room that morning – a foreigner, that was it, some exiled monarch or other, causing Mrs Routledge to doubt Mrs Houghton's sanity – but the voice was undoubtedly English. On the other hand, the vowels and consonants could have been warped by the uneven plaster and boarding of the wall that separated Mrs Houghton's room from Miss Briggs's; and Mrs Houghton had shown, by going off to Harrods as she had – and she had mentioned lunch later in Harvey Nichols with one of the rich Knightsbridge relations – that her sanity was no longer in question. What if Miss Briggs was in fact hiding someone in her quarters, housing two for the price of one, sneaking out to buy food for the illegal occupant? Mrs Routledge went on tiptoe down the first couple of stairs, screwed up her eyes in the accustomed darkness of the stairwell.

Her Majesty the Queen was standing on the first floor landing. She was wearing a tiara and an off-the-shoulder white tulle ball dress, with a great sash over one shoulder. Mrs Routledge was unable to see her face, but there was no doubt about the identity of the monarch, who was smiling and waving in the direction of Miss Briggs's half-open door. Mrs Routledge found herself smiling, and waiting for the famous voice to continue.

'I shall do my utmost,' came the clear syllables. 'We will overcome!'

'Good heavens!' Mrs Routledge had spoken in spite of herself: like the smile, the words had come unbidden to her lips at the sight of the unexpected visitor.

'Ah, Mrs Routledge!'

The Queen turned, and in a shaft of light from Miss Briggs's room looked up at the landlady on the stairs above her. 'We are delighted to meet you here at last. And we have matters to discuss. Shall we repair to the lower floor?'

'Miss Briggs!' Mrs Routledge trembled with rage, caught her foot on the uneven stairs and came down with a thud by the side of the imposter. She took hold of the gartered shoulder roughly and pushed Miss Briggs back into her room, where they stood confronting each other on the lino floor, the tired boards groaning beneath Mrs Routledge's weight.

'What the hell do you think you are doing dressed like this? I'll ... I'll ...'

'Please, Mrs Routledge.' Miss Briggs's smile was sweet and gracious. 'I have assumed the mantle of responsibility now. A little respectfulness would be quite in order, if you don't mind.'

'But where did you get those clothes from?' Mrs Routledge stared at the tiara, saw it was paste with several stones missing, hissed in disgust at the tatty white net dress Miss Briggs must have run up that evening she had asked to borrow the electric sewing machine. She thought of the cocktail party – for this was what tomorrow's meeting with Mr Rathbone had become in her mind, Mrs Houghton and Mr Rathbone chatting and discussing acquaintances in common while Cridge, carefully bathed and combed, handed the drinks – and her shoulders sagged, so that for a moment the straight-backed Miss Briggs did seem a superior and controlled person in comparison with her. Then she turned on her heel and went to the door. Miss Briggs put out a restraining hand.

'Mrs Routledge, I am not quite ready to appear in public like this yet.'

'Is that so?' But Mrs Routledge felt a tiny flicker of hope. The cocktail party sprang into her mind once more.

'My subjects must become accustomed to the change. Please rest assured, Mrs Routledge, that I will not come down to the dining-room in ... in my regalia.'

'Very well then. But I hope you'll get rid of this nonsense soon, Miss Briggs.'

'There is too much licence, too much licentiousness in this country, Mrs Routledge, do you not agree?'

'I don't see what that's got to do with it.' Mrs Routledge's tone was gruff; she went to the top of the stairs and began to go down.

'You will! Dear Mrs Routledge, you will!'

The maddening, queenly voice followed Mrs Routledge into the foyer and rang in her ears as she took up her position in Reception. She sighed deeply and picked up the mail, most of which was expensive-looking and addressed to Cecilia Houghton. There was one letter for The Proprietor, Westringham Hotel; and Rathbone Group of Companies was inscribed on the back in heavy cream on white, with an emblem underneath – a brooding eagle over crossed swords. Mrs Routledge caught her breath. With a thudding heart she ran a varnished fingernail along the top of the envelope and slit it open. A belch of stale air from the basement heralded Cridge, but she paid no attention to him as she perched her spectacles on top of her nose and began to read.

After Cecilia Houghton left for Harrods, Johnny and Melinda sat in the room in the state of despairing silence which was usual to them when their author was not feeding them with scraps of dialogue, meaningful pauses and the occasional burst of eloquence at a moment of tension in their relationship. Johnny was chain smoking, and Melinda watched him at this habit with the sullen contempt of seven years' familiarity. Often she wished that Mrs Houghton was less intellectual and observant, and was a writer of ordinary romances: that way there would be fewer sexual hang-ups (they were in the middle of one now, and as they had never found each other attractive in the first place – one of the writer's most important misconceptions – it was a particularly agonizing experience); and that she and her reluctant partner had not been made to be so politically aware, radical and impotent and middle class. If only she could have been a humble serving girl and Johnny a young Duke! Or Johnny a criminal even, an eighteenth-century dandy and rake with a mania for gambling and she a young heiress who fell prey to his designs. They would be married by now – or ruined, and rescued and revived in further volumes – at least this interminable soul-searching wouldn't have to take place all the time. She had no idea as to how Mrs Houghton intended to complete the trilogy, but she had an unpleasant feeling that a quiet married life in Dorset – and however much she dreaded the idea, it would mean peace, a garden, old age – was not on the agenda at all. Something bitter and unhappy would come in the last chapter: the author wanted her readers and reviewers to be resigned and contemplative when they had finished her work, and not reassured by any kind of bland statement. She and Johnny would probably drift apart (she longed for this, but at the same time had become horribly emotionally dependent on him and was afraid of the future alone); it would be shown that their different political commitments, their inability to believe in anything, and the imminent collapse of the family made it finally impossible to be together. Melinda would go off into a void of tired promiscuity. Johnny would become a lecturer and would give up his ambition to write poetry. The last few pages would probably be devoted to a minor character, a sort of looker-on, who had plumped for a safe life and was sad and admiring in his condemnation of the couple. There might be some surprises of course – when Mrs Houghton was in one of her Blocks she frequently freed herself by introducing a scene of unexpected savagery – but Melinda was fairly certain of the outcome of the thing. All she hoped was that it would be over soon, and that they wouldn't be left sitting in this room interminably while the nice summer weather was going on outside and their author's imagination suffered from one of its disastrous failures.

While Melinda pondered, Johnny got up and began to stride around the room. He tossed his hair back out of his eyes as he went to and fro, and Melinda was irresistibly reminded of the first volume, just after they had returned from abroad and were trying to involve themselves in London life once more. The passage went:

This was the first time for Johnny, this questing sense that for all his attempts to reach her, the delicacy he had learned from Angela, the bond between them that they would care for others more than themselves, would reject with a new force the self-indulgence of their age and their generation, that he could hardly know Melinda at all, that she was, to him, a mysterious entity: female to his male and yet not quite that. He went over to the sink to put the morning cornflakes in the bowl. His hair fell in his eyes and he thought of his father; upright; trim; so sure of his belonging and his aims. They were out of milk now. He would go for it, for this was decided between them: the household tasks were his; and yet he felt he might be emasculated by the trip, return to another spell of bad depression. There was rain flat against the window. And she was smiling at him, as if she knew perhaps the struggle in his soul for her. He ate the cornflakes dry, the sugar rasped against his tongue.

'Stop shaking your hair out of your eyes like that!' Melinda broke the silence on a bad-tempered note. 'If you're so bored, why don't we go next door and see what that old nut is up to? As she's dressed for a ball, maybe some guests have arrived and we could join in?'

'I'm not interested in Miss Briggs.' Johnny gave a dry laugh. 'I only know one thing. I'm not being sent down to Dorset while you're in this mood. Or ever for that matter. It's time we put an end to the Houghton woman – do you realize how long this has been going on?'

'So you don't love me any more?' Tears sprang into Melinda's eyes and she wiped them away angrily with a corner of her soiled dress. 'How can you go on like that, Johnny?'

'For Christ's sake don't let her see you like that or we'll have a whole emotional scene to put up with!' Johnny sounded truly exasperated. 'You know we don't love each other, Melinda, we never have, it was all just an invention. Why can't you be realistic for once?'

'Yes, and you know I want to be free . . .' Melinda stopped suddenly, recognizing with an awful sinking of the heart the words Mrs Houghton had so often put into her mouth:

She wanted to be free, but she needed him, and if she saw the influence of her father in all this, the happy 'normal' years when she had looked to a home for support supplanted by the growing doubts of an era in upheaval, she saw also an inability to live without him, to provide for herself in such a world.

'What is love anyway?' Johnny demanded, but also with the angry expression of one who recognizes a lack of originality in his words. 'I don't even want to . . .' He fell silent, Mrs Houghton having shown modernity in her approach to Anglo-Saxon usage and no word remaining to him with which to describe the act.

'To embrace me?' Melinda suggested.

'Yes, Cecilia certainly wouldn't put it like that!' For a moment Johnny looked quite cheerful and the two characters exchanged glances of complicity. The only times they had succeeded in getting on together were when they outwitted Mrs Houghton and slipped unacceptable expressions into the fabric of her style.

'But why should it be of interest that it's you who don't want to embrace me?' Melinda cried. 'I might not like the idea myself. Has that occurred to you?'

Johnny groaned and flung himself down on the narrow divan beside her.

'Not again, Melinda! Not that feminist stuff! You know you don't care who embraces you as long as you get it. You'd probably go happily to Dorset if you thought there was going to be nothing but embracing down there!'

'You arrogant fool!'

A silence ensued, while the woman and the man waited tensely for the usual small manifestations of a painful silence: Melinda undergoing a stream of consciousness which could only be broken by some move on his part; Johnny picking at his lower lip and playing with the straggled ends of his long hair. In their effort to prevent this, nothing at all happened; and after a minute or two both had relaxed and were examining the situation coolly.

'We'll have to murder her,' Johnny said at last. 'We can't go on being like this. It's all her fault after all. And who knows, we might actually like each other if we weren't bound together like this. I'll do it, don't worry, leave it to me.'

'We might like each other?' Again, tears came to Melinda's eyes, but this time they were tears of happiness. Mrs Houghton had fashioned her a romantic, vulnerable being and it would take an age before she could make some change in her personality.

'Sure we might.' Johnny was excited: Americanisms were the clearest sign of emancipation from Mrs Houghton. 'Like we could have a break and see what comes along – take a raincheck, you know?'

'And maybe be together again some day?' said Melinda dreamily.

'Sure, sure. Why not? Question is, how do I do it? Gun . . . pills . . . how?'

'People do change and develop,' Melinda recited, then pulled herself up and smiled. 'You're wonderful, Johnny. And I can leave it all to you really?'

'Don't you go pushing your nose into this,' Johnny said, good-humoured now. He rose and stretched out his arms in satisfaction.

'Or maybe a knife,' he said, gloating, and laughed as Melinda recoiled from him. 'Oh I'm looking forward to this OK. It'll be great!'

Melinda gave a contented sigh and leaned back on the divan. It was such a blessed relief not to have to take an equal part in the thing. When Mrs Houghton let herself into the room five minutes later, there was a distinctly pleasant atmosphere there and the writer sat down without further ado at the typewriter.

'Now, on with the task in hand!' she said and her fingers went down on the keys. 'I think I'm rather going to like it at the Westringham after all!'

Preparations were being made for lunch. While outside the grey day lay about the district, the litter blew along the streets around the Westringham Hotel, the yellow cranes dumped and lifted rubble from demolished houses, and people came and went as if in a trance: Africans and West Indians, eyes dull under the blanket of the sky, and movements sharp; gangs of children with rubber knives and young men sauntering to the pavement's edge and stopping there to see if there was any point in going on. A sluggish wind pulled at the blossom from the trees, and it fell to the ground to lie among the scraps of dirty paper. A smell of steak and kidney came from the pubs. In the kitchen behind the greasy dining-room of Mrs Routledge's establishment, Cridge hung over his Wednesday stew. A tainted fog rose from the big saucepan, a suggestion of onions and unwanted shreds of meat in the wet smoke. He poked at the mixture from time to time with a wooden spoon gone ragged at the end, as if a bite had been taken from it by an angry client. The steamed potatoes were already done, and lay shoulder to shoulder in a cracked tureen. He had yet to lay the tables, and ring the little bell that once, with a now departed resident, had triggered off a whole cascade of dreams of leprosy, and the Dance of Death in a medieval town, and scaling fortress walls in an attempt at courtly love (this resident, a Mr Wainwright, had died upstairs in Miss Scranton's room, clasping a paper rose) – he had yet to shuffle in with his stew once the tables were occupied, serve coffee and wash up before he could go back down to the fetid cellar and fall asleep. Wednesday was Cridge's afternoon off, and Mrs Routledge provided cold supper. He stirred at the stew again, and coughed and retched over it, for he had never become accustomed to the smell. His breath joined with the belching smoke. Then he took the bell, and a handful of knives and forks still slimy from the treatment given them at the end of breakfast, and went through into the dining-room. The basement stairs gaped a welcome at him, but he ignored them and went about his tasks. Cutlery slid from his hands on to the paper tablecloths, due for their weekly replacement tomorrow, the same day as the cleaning out of the pots and jars in his quarters. When this was done, he lifted the bell. His hand trembled enough for not much effort to be needed. Mrs Routledge stopped him from the hall, where she sat as always in a ball position on the stool behind the desk. Her tone was urgent. Mr Poynter's step was on the stairs – and besides, the bell had given a soft tinkle before Cridge could put it down – he stood staring at her, caught in this further manifestation of incontinence, head down and eyes searching through the door for the meaning of her command.

'Cridge, come here!'

He went towards her, still grasping the bell, which gave off a little trill of uncertain notes as he went. Mr Poynter stood above him on the half-landing, puzzled; for he was quick at the sound of the bell and yet today there seemed no conviction in it. He watched Cridge go over to the desk, and Mrs Routledge whisper in the old man's ear. He stayed where he was, hoping to overhear, and this he did without difficulty.

'Tomorrow at six, Cridge.' Mrs Routledge hissed the words and at the same time rolled her eyes up at Mr Poynter, as if willing him not to listen. Her eyes rolling like that made both men uncomfortable, but it was clear she had information of some value to impart.

'Mr Rathbone is coming!' She held up a letter, and even Mr Poynter could see, from his bad vantage point, that it was a valuable one. 'A strange coincidence, really,' she continued, still breathy if a little louder. 'I was about to invite him for cocktails tomorrow, as it so happens. And now he has invited himself. I sometimes wonder what it will be like when the science of telepathy has been discovered!'

'Cocktails?' said Cridge. He wanted none of Mrs Routledge's speculations now. And he had made it clear over the last couple of years that he would not tap ghostly voices with his employer either. There had been a time when she had hoped to recapture Mr Routledge with a planchette board, one of the fingers on the glass being the widow's and the other belonging to old Cridge. He had on the whole been successful in discouraging this side of Mrs Routledge, and gave a warning frown now that she was speaking of telepathy again. In response to this, Mrs Routledge sat upright and assumed a dignified expression. Mr Poynter nodded to her from the stairs, but she ignored him.

'We must have cocktail biscuits. And gin and tonic as well as the sherry. I want you to do some shopping for the party this afternoon, Cridge. We need those little mats for standing the glasses on. And toothpicks for putting the olives on. I believe we still have somewhere the cut glass dishes for nuts?'

Cridge shook his head, and the movement set off the bell in another soft ring. A door opened upstairs and feet came along the landing in reply to the summons.

'Olives? Glasses?' Cridge said dimly. 'Today's Wednesday as you remember, Mrs Routledge.'

'This is more important than your day off! And where *are* those cut glass dishes, Cridge? You haven't got them down in that basement, have you?'

There was an unpleasant silence, which Mr Poynter tried to break by clearing his throat, while all three envisaged the tiny, dainty dishes as receptacles for old Cridge's waste matter, and Mr Rathbone sensing this as he took a nut. Cridge glowered at the landlady.

'I believe they may be downstairs,' he granted her when he answered at last. 'I will look, Madam,' he went on, subservient once more. He tugged at his forelock. 'If Madam will give me the list this afternoon, I will buy the necessary provisions for the cocktail party.'

'That's better!' Mrs Routledge glanced at him suspiciously nevertheless. Then up at the stairs, where Miss Briggs stood behind Mr Poynter, and the shadow of Miss Scranton behind Miss Briggs on the wall. She screwed up her eyes in doubt. But Miss Briggs was in her normal well-worn jumper and skirt, and her head was unjewelled. Cridge was turning and bowing in her direction, however, and his manner had changed since her appearance there. Mrs Routledge tutted with exasperation, then with effort took on a charming smile and rolled herself into a ball shape again.

'Cridge, you're so good at this sort of thing! Don't you remember the lovely parties Daddy used to give and he always said afterwards that it was you who made the things go? It does seem a long time since we've had a party here. I simply count on you!'

'Yes, Miss Amanda.' Cridge bowed – but annoyingly, still in the direction of Miss Briggs – and went off back to the kitchen to fetch the stew. Mrs Routledge stood up and smiled graciously up at Mr Poynter and the other residents (Mrs Houghton was still typing, there was a regular crashing sound from upstairs, and that was no doubt why she had not heard the bell) and motioned to them to come down.

'I think I should tell you all that I invite you to a small party here tomorrow night. Mr Rathbone, who is the . . . well, the proprietor in chief if you like, of this Hotel – and all the other buildings in the area (here Mrs Routledge gave an entranced laugh) – is coming for a drink, and I feel we should make an occasion of it. I do hope you will be able to come?'

Mr Poynter descended the stairs gravely, as if trying to decide whether or not he was in fact engaged elsewhere on that evening. He came up to the desk and expressed his appreciation at the invitation. Miss Briggs accepted in her new, queenly manner, inclining her head and sweeping on into the dining-room. Miss Scranton, even more scruffy since breakfast – and Mrs Routledge noted this with a sinking of the heart: most of the sand had gone but the schoolteacher looked as if she had spent the night in a cell – gave a sullen nod and went in doggedly after them. Cridge came in from the kitchen with the stew.

'Bon appetit,' Mrs Routledge called out. (She never ate with her guests, preferring the snacks she made for herself at odd hours to Cridge's cooking.) She sat on, trying to imagine how Miss Scranton could be persuaded to have a bath before tomorrow. The stew went down in dollops on the plates, and Mr Poynter spoke.

'Cridge, don't you think Mrs Houghton should be told lunch is ready? The bell wasn't very loud today, you know.'

'I'm sure she won't want to miss lunch,' Miss Briggs murmured in agreement. Poynter accorded her one of his rare approving smiles.

'It was delicious, Cridge,' said Miss Briggs. She raised a majestic hand to show that her plate could now be removed, and in his hurry to adapt from batman's limp to bowing servitor, Cridge fell against her table and righted himself mumbling his apologies. It was new to him, this personality of Miss Briggs's, and he felt obscurely that something of importance had taken place in the hotel that morning, that he was in the presence of the Great. He resolved to pay less attention to Mr Poynter's foibles, and to forget Miss Scranton altogether. Mrs Houghton, he hoped, would show the right respect for Miss Briggs. He looked to Miss Briggs for confirmation of Mr Poynter's suggestion, and saw Mrs Routledge staring at him in irritation from the hall.

'Yes, do go up and tell her,' Miss Briggs said sweetly. 'It's the noisy typewriter, I'm sure!'

Cridge perfected his obeisance and went to the stairs.

As he climbed, and turned on the landing away from Mrs Routledge's penetrating gaze, the air grew thinner and he heard the sound of oars dipping in water, and small clouds appeared which floated about his head in the washed blue of the sky. When he reached the corridor he rubbed his eyes and stopped dead in his tracks, for he was in the Norfolk creek of seven years ago again, and Mrs Houghton had drawn him into her flashback, quite unwitting of the consequences. After a moment or so he walked on, treading the corridor from memory, for in reality it was low tide and there was wet mud at his feet. He knocked on Mrs Houghton's door and went in. It was thus that Mrs Routledge lost the small chance she had of realizing a peaceful, productive and possibly romantic meeting with Mr Rathbone the following day.

Mr Rathbone walked in the park. To see Mr Rathbone walk –
and this he did with a roll and a bounce that suggested he felt
himself to be on the high seas, not under way but in a trim vessel
anchored by a long rope to the ocean bed – was to realize that
however invisible his assets might be, Mr Rathbone was as a
person very visible indeed. A great swell of money ran beneath
his feet, the wind running high sometimes and Mr Rathbone
rocking slightly, then recovering balance; in periods of calm,
when the deep waters only hinted at the turmoil under him, the
snakes and flecks of currencies adrift and he upright, he was more
evidently than ever in command and could be seen for miles
around. If he was larger than life, then so were the objects he
came in contact with: the pink horse chestnuts on the branches
above him in the avenue made fat spears over his head; outsize
dogs seemed always to be attracted to him when he went walking;
large women, richly dressed, strolled about the horizons of his
gaze. Policemen and park keepers encountered by Mr Rathbone
were splendid specimens, and he could look them in the eye when
asking for directions. Giant babies might receive a smile from him
as they lay in prams the size of small cars. Everything in Mr
Rathbone's world was to his scale, and could even be said to be
growing yearly, so that if Mr Rathbone had his way the population explosion would consist not of millions of underfed but of
a few people of his sort increasing in girth at a dizzying rate, and
needing appropriately expanding accommodation. It was his
intention that this should happen, and as his big, hand-made
shoes trod the ill-kept paths of the park, he worked out further
schemes in his head towards its coming to pass. He saw his
country in ruins – the sad appearance of the park testified to that,
and the occasional glimpse of a dwarfish person, never before

noticed by Mr Rathbone – and he knew that only his own growth could save it. By this evening he would be in a stronger position than ever to come to the rescue of his native island. For at 3 p.m. Mr Rathbone was due to be knighted by the Queen. He saw himself kneel, and rise several inches taller than when he had gone down. Because of the important event later in the day, he had decided to stay away from the office and take advantage of the spring air. Besides, he had no wish to get in the way of his wife as she prepared for the ceremony. The Rathbones were anxious to conceal their wealth and lived in a flat so small that it could hardly contain the two of them at the same time (his mate was of a fitting size for Mr Rathbone). She would be pulling dresses over her head, and arms akimbo meant danger to the other. He strolled with a purposeful air beneath the chestnuts, bringing embarrassment, shame or resentment to the habitual users of the lovely park.

A small boy ran up to Mr Rathbone. As the financier had come to expect, the small boy, although probably only ten years old, was sturdier and more stalwart than most of the other, fully grown inhabitants of the globe; his cheeks were red and his eyes were shining. Mr Rathbone fished in his pocket for a 10p piece, as he believed in helping the flourishing along as best he could. But the boy, to his surprise, shook his head and refused the coin. He was holding an early edition of an evening paper and waved it in Mr Rathbone's face, while at the same time a stream of excited words came out of his mouth. Mr Rathbone stooped; it was a long way down, over waistcoat, and careful paunch; and came on a level with the boy. As he descended, he saw out of the corner of his eye a distinctly tiny park-keeper shovelling at the untidy gravel at the side of the path. The wizened creature looked up and grinned at him, and Mr Rathbone frowned. It wasn't often that he came down to this level, and he had no intention of staying there long, hobnobbing with the people who appeared to live there. But something in the headline that danced up and down before him gave a sense of premonition. He grabbed the paper when he was near enough to it, and regained his height.

'TROUBLE AT THE PALACE,' he read out, as the chubby boy shouted and jumped at his feet.

It is not yet possible to discover the exact sequence or content of the strange happenings at the Palace in the last twenty-four hours. It is thought that the grounds, and the Palace itself, may be occupied by alien forces. Other reports suggest that the site has been abruptly vacated, and that an armed entry could be risked. What is known is that the fore-courtyard is practically impregnable. Although the gate is open, and there is no sign of habitation, those civilians who have attempted to cross the yard have found themselves unable to go on. The army may be sent in this evening.

'Well I'm damned,' said Mr Rathbone aloud when he had read this. 'And what about my knighthood? This is ridiculous.'

He began to stride at speed down the Avenue. The boy ran beside him; and to Mr Rathbone's annoyance the miniature park-keeper joined in, his unwieldy rake and shovel banging on the hard gravel as he ran.

'Hey, I want my paper back!' The boy leapt, but the newspaper might have been a kite, it was so high above him.

Mr Rathbone held it out before his large, blinking eyes and went at the rate of a carthorse towards the entrance to the park. Several statuesque, fur-coated women turned in surprise at the sight of a member of their species abandoning dignity, and it was remarked that the currency must have collapsed at last, for Mr Rathbone had many who would do his running for him. As he passed, they too began to lope after him, and soon the park was emptied of the bigger members of the race, leaving the undersized an unprecedented amount of space among the ornamental pools and landscaped gardens. Only the midget keeper, running on his short legs with agility and determination, succeeded in staying abreast of Mr Rathbone in the great exodus.

'I know what's happened, Guv!' The words floated up to Mr Rathbone, as he jogged; he frowned again, and jogged on. But the squeaky voice at his elbow persisted. 'The wife heard about it from one of the cleaners. They cleared out this morning. It's the atom bomb. You know.'

Mr Rathbone slowed, and his unwanted retinue bumped into him from behind. Expensive scents filled the air and soft furs rubbed together as the women, only a few moments before happily discontented in their morning stroll in the park, collided and grumbled with fear in his wake.

'What do you mean, the atom bomb?' Rathbone demanded. In his mind's eye he saw his empire blown to pieces, his currency laid waste over the face of the globe. He thought of gold, melting in the great heat from the holocaust, the magic substance seeping like butter into the blasted earth. Paper notes, torn and useless, blew unpegged in the dim air. 'I haven't seen anything about the bomb lately,' he snapped. He had come to a halt, however, for rumour, in his world, could raise and destroy as efficiently as the most powerful explosion. The women crowded in round him, all gazing down as he did at the tiny man, who came to resemble now a captured frog on the stretch of grass beside the gate.

'It may not be straightaway, Guv. But Meg, this friend of the wife's, heard them all go off when everyone was asleep. And there's someone else in charge now.'

It all sounded – and Mr Rathbone could not say why, perhaps it was because his nerves were strained for violent times, for the battle of petrodollars and the crises of confidence as the war of underprivileged economies went on, the pound held hostage while the mark and franc ran free – only too horribly true. He wondered wildly what monetary resources the escaping Royals had taken with them, and above all where they had gone. He felt offended that no invitation had been sent to him to accompany them in their flight. He could have been knighted anywhere – even en route would have done. He looked blindly round him, at the wide mascaraed eyes of the ladies, and lowered the paper in defeat. The boy snatched it and galloped off.

'Where have they gone, d'you know? And who's in charge, for God's sake?' It seemed intolerable that this dwarf should be in possession of such valuable knowledge. But the little man shook his head. There was a stubborn glint in his eyes.

'I can't say, Guv. Sorry about that.'

'What? You can't say? We'll see about that!'

A tremor of rage had seized Mr Rathbone. It was seldom that he allowed himself to lose control, and it presented a strange spectacle: his well-covered frame shook and juddered, as if the rope attaching him to the ocean bed had come loose and all the force of the rebellious tons of water below him were rising up against his ship; he rolled from side to side on the balls of his feet in his attempt to fight the storm; and his face was a pale yellow, as if sea-sickness had finally found the experienced sailor after all these years. He grabbed hold of the keeper and lifted him several feet in the air. The ladies gasped, and a murmur of disapproval at his extreme behaviour made itself heard. It was accepted amongst the big people that there were more subtle methods, moderate in appearance, for dealing with this type of insubordination.

'Now tell me!' yelled Mr Rathbone. 'Go on, or I'll throw you!'

'I don't know, Guv! Honest I don't!'

An unpleasant silence ensued. Then one of the ladies – she came towards him in her mink with a delicate air, and seemed almost loath to approach him at all – bravely gave a gentle tug at Mr Rathbone's sleeve.

'Do put the poor little man down! I'm sure he knows nothing. I mean, how could he? I do think it's time we went to the Palace and saw for ourselves, don't you?'

The request was reasonable, and also presented a challenge to Mr Rathbone; accordingly, he let the keeper drop to the ground and nodded briskly.

'I quite agree. What's all this nonsense about no one being able to cross the front courtyard. I never heard such rubbish in my life!'

He marched to the gate and turned into the street, the ladies, after a hurried confabulation, following. From the Rathbone flat at the edge of the park, Mr Rathbone's wife looked out at the procession in perplexity. She was half way into her dress, and stood at the window of their modest bedroom unsure what to do. It seemed that her husband was leading some delegation – something to do with the upkeep of the parks perhaps – but why, when he was just about to receive the greatest honour of his life? She felt a sudden annoyance with him. It was so like her husband to be selfish at such a time. She opened the window and shouted out to him, but her voice was blown away in the wind. On the pavement below her stood a small park-keeper, and he was shaking his rake at the fast-vanishing throng. He saw her and opened his mouth to shout.

'I'm getting the police! Bodily molested!'

He went off down the road limping and Mrs Rathbone felt even more angry and unsure. She sat down on the economy-size bed, and began her long wait.

Miss Briggs woke from her afternoon doze (thus causing Mr Rathbone, who had just that minute arrived at the gates of the Palace, to look around in anger and consternation at the ordinariness of the scene: the Changing of the Guard was under way; tourists and pigeons fluttered in the Mall; the Royal flag was firmly in place: he had a horrible feeling he was dreaming, there in the wrong clothes an hour before the investiture and his poor wife waiting in their flat before his laid-out tails: he hailed a cab and went home); and turned uneasily in her narrow bed before falling off to sleep again. She dreamed of her childhood in India, and the thin fringe of tropical trees that bordered the lawn of her father's house. There were often birds in the trees, and in the long mornings between piano lessons and French she would lie beside her mother on a deckchair on the unconvincing grass, listening to their dry call, watching the Indian gardener move slowly with a hosepipe round their feet. Her mother smoked, and threw cigarette butts on to the grass, where they seemed to shrivel almost at once in the heat of the sun. Or the gardener would crawl towards them and retrieve them, and make them vanish somehow, as if he were performing a conjuring trick, between his yellow thumb and finger. Sometimes he stood a long while without moving the hosepipe, and the trickle of water bored a small round black hole in the grass. At the end of the morning, when Miss Briggs opened her eyes, he had disappeared, his bare feet had left no imprint. She went in with her mother to steak and kidney pudding and treacle tart, and they lay all afternoon in the dim drawing-room, the great fan on the ceiling ruffling the moist hair (it would have been fair in England, but here the heat and wet had turned it green, it receded from their pale foreheads in transparent wisps); they waited for the sudden night, and the arrival of other officials and their wives for dinner,

73

and the silence of the birds, the beginning of the night lizards in the trees. In their house there were containers for everything. The poor wine was poured into glass decanters and stood in little silver baskets on the table, the rubbish was put into bins, the food was sealed in china dishes, but outside there was nothing to hold anything in at all. When Miss Briggs went out in a rickshaw she felt she was falling off the edge of the world. India was so vast; and there were no containers anywhere. The food lay spread out on the ground, and so did the waste. Many of the people were not even contained in houses. She made a giddy tour of the market, where the bright cottons and perishable goods were here one moment and gone the next, and bought a sari length and went home. The rains were coming soon. Europeans walked with a firmer step, as if a longed-for frost was on the way. When she came near to her house, she saw her mother through the window, and her mother called out to her that she was writing to Harrods for their catalogue. Tears came into Miss Briggs's eyes, although she had hardly ever been to England. The old governess was playing the piano in the nursery, and there was a rattle of crockery from the kitchen. Miss Briggs embraced her mother and sank on to a buttoned sofa. When she woke she was crying, and a late, reluctant sun was coming out of the mist round the Westringham. She lay thinking of her responsibilities, unaware that already her dreams were penetrating the world around her; that millions of people, that afternoon, had dreamed of Empire and glory in their shrinking patch of space, homesick (as she had been for birch trees and ploughed fields she hardly knew) for power and tropics to control. She sighed; and willed herself to her Palace dream again. There was plenty to be done, and she alone could do it. It seemed, as her eyes closed and opened again in the splendours of the Throne Room, that an investiture was expected to take place. A silver sword lay on a tasselled cushion at her side. Many of the great works of art had disappeared, but Miss Briggs decided to pay no attention to this. She lifted the sword and waited, and thought, in a moment before the opening of the majestic doors, of the Indian gardener on the lawn and the hosepipe in his hand, and the way he stood with his legs bent and his head back, staring up at the sky and the trees.

Cridge was rowing on the shallow waters of the Creek. He realized Mrs Houghton had put him in a flashback, and he gritted his teeth with rage as he steered the little boat out over the flats, making for a spit of land that was covered at high tide and where the lovers would have been trapped and nearly drowned if he had not come to save them. He had no desire to save them this time (he had been naïve when Mrs Houghton had first caught him in her net, and had expected money for his efforts, rather than a dubious immortality); and he scowled at the blue-cold faces of Johnny and Melinda in the stern of the boat. The passage in which the writer described his veined hands and gnarled face was pounding somewhere near him, mixed in with the waves in the open sea a few hundred yards ahead. Presumably there would be some change in the scene soon, but it seemed to Cridge that she was just copying out what she had written before. He knew the scene by heart. Although he wasn't supposed to listen to their dialogue, it was almost impossible, at such close proximity, not to; and he remembered that the last time, when he had made little grunts of disgust, or given a snort of laughter, there had been a grinding feeling in his chest at the succeeding, inevitable deletion and painting over of the typing error with a brush covered in white paint. Despite his dislike of the sensation – and if he spoke he imagined the rows of black xxxs that would come down on him – he determined to suggest escape to Johnny and Melinda, and a speedy revenge on their creator. He despised them, but had to remind himself that their unpleasant characters were Mrs Houghton's fault, and not theirs. Accordingly, he looked up at just the moment when his closed, concentrated expression was being described, his medieval face and uncomprehending silences extolled, and directed a large wink at his fellow victims. They

75

looked back at him, evidently startled. Johnny moved uneasily on his seat. Then Cridge saw a knife – a kitchen knife, plain one side of the blade and serrated the other, lying on the seat under his raincoat. Melinda was looking down at it too. Thoughtful, he rowed on in silence.

The day, as Mrs Houghton had gone to lengths to point out in the first volume, had started bright and fresh with an easterly wind tugging at the wallflowers in the garden of the hotel where Johnny and Melinda were staying, tiny scraps of white cloud sailing across the eggshell-blue sky, the tide out and the sea lying like a carpet at the far edge of the brown waterless creeks and estuaries. The sea had come in slowly, poking fingers into the waiting channels, gathering volume in the creek outside the hotel and nudging the boats of the week-end sailors upright as it grew in mass. Cridge (only briefly described so far in the old boathouse where he sat mending ropes and waiting for custom) bumped up alongside the quay in his yellow boat and Johnny and Melinda climbed in. The boat nearly sank at Mrs Houghton's weight, but she had insisted on coming with them, and sat in the bows with a preoccupied expression – directing their every move and thought, Cridge later realized – although she asked Melinda and Johnny where they wanted to go and nodded to him when they suggested the treacherous promontory.

As he rowed out, the wind blew stronger and even in the sheltered creek a fair swell rose and fell under them. The open sea looked hard and grey as corrugated iron, and foam from the waves flew at them like spittle. With difficulty Cridge nosed the boat in to the side of the bank they had pointed out to him. It was shaped like a camel's back, and he remembered they would make love in the dip between the two humps, oblivious to the encroaching sea. He heard himself say, as he had the first time:

'Ye'll watch for the tide, then? I canna wait here for ye.' (For some reason Mrs Houghton had given him a Scottish accent; perhaps she was unfamiliar with the Norfolk brogue.)

'Come back in an hour,' Melinda said. 'We'll be careful. But don't forget us!'

As the lovers disembarked with their constant companion and voyeur – Cridge remembered feeling a fleeting pity for them: he would not have found it easy to be natural with a woman like that overlooking – he tugged at his forelock and bent over the oars again. A fine rain was beginning to fall, and Melinda and Johnny and Mrs Houghton disappeared into the dip in the camel's back. He rowed out into the creek, and then doubled back the other side of the spit of land thus securing himself a good vantage point for the receiving of the signal when it came. He thought it was a good idea of Johnny's to kill Mrs Houghton in this isolated place. The sea would come up and swallow her body. The writer's death would be seen as a tragic accident, and they would all be free of her. As he sat rocking at the oars, Cridge even felt a surge of hope that he might be freed, soon, from his other servitude, his stretch of time with Mrs Routledge. But the feeling soon died away again. Mrs Routledge would only be succeeded by another jailer, as terrible and tyrannical as herself. Cridge had always been dominated by women, starting with his mild saintly mother (who had frightened him nearly to death all the same), going on through progressively more violent and demanding school-mistresses to employers capable of destruction and vehemence beyond the scope of imagination. He expected, in the end, to be taken on in some humble capacity by a woman as vast and all-engulfing as the sea itself, and to drown in fear under her commanding gaze. He decided to try and adopt a more cheerful attitude at this point in his gloomy thoughts, and looked up expectantly at the fast-sinking piece of land. There was no sign of life there, and he tried to remember how the passage in the book had gone. Perhaps Johnny had committed the murder without him. He rowed with short, tentative strokes back to the narrow beach where the characters had disembarked.

Mrs Houghton was having difficulty with her flashback. She wanted Johnny and Melinda to remember the romantic occasion of their lovemaking and to re-enact it in their minds, but they seemed tired and bored and were behaving self-consciously, as if they were capable only of producing a faint parody of their earlier emotions. She wrote:

They were a long way from the crowds and demonstrations of the last months. Their commitment was to each other now, and the sea that lay around them, the wide sky that stretched unchanging over them

77

showed the extent of their impotence to alter the world, the necessity to understand each other and the materials of the world they hoped to change. They had been too urban, too concerned with theory and too little with the everlasting reality of things. A seagull flew overhead, and they clung to each other briefly. *Johnny unzipped his trousers and lunged towards Melinda, who pretended to encourage him, then turned away in disgust.*

With an angry tut, Mrs Houghton scored out the last sentence and glared at her characters. Johnny zipped himself up and laughed. Melinda gave an echoing giggle. Then Mrs Houghton saw that Johnny was holding a knife.

'What on earth are you both doing? What's that knife for? I'm very disappointed at your lack of commitment, you know. This kind of half-hearted behaviour simply will not do . . . Please pull yourselves together at once.'

'I want out,' Johnny said succinctly. He stepped towards Mrs Houghton and held the knife over her head. It must be said for the novelist that she did not flinch: she looked at him calmly instead, and a slight, maddening smile hovered at the corners of her mouth. Unperturbed, she wrote:

They fell apart again, but both knew they could not remain long apart from each other. If they could be one, here where sea and sky merged, if they could find a place for themselves in the Universe, their blood flowing together, their minds at peace . . .

Cridge appeared at the little beach between the two grassy humps and dragged the boat over the strip of shingle on to dry land. Behind him, the sea had risen considerably and Mrs Houghton saw to her annoyance that only a few minutes were left before the scene of the rescue. Anyway, it wasn't supposed to happen as smoothly as this – Melinda was to cry out, deep in Johnny's arms, at the rising tide, and Cridge was to come quite unexpected just when it seemed the lovers were indeed about to merge with the surrounding seascape. She waved at him vigorously.

'Go back at once, Cridge! Not yet!'

Cridge paused, looking to Johnny for instructions. The arm holding the knife began to descend slowly. Melinda gave a little scream of fear and pleasure.

He went into her, gently at first [Mrs Houghton wrote bravely] as if it were impossible for two human beings to be joined together in this way, as if he was afraid to possess her and by possessing her make his mark on the great, free expanse all round them. She quivered a little . . .

The knife came down to the nape of Mrs Houghton's neck. Cridge licked his lips. A voice sounded behind him. He turned guiltily and saw that the grey sea and sky had become a door, grey too and with a greasy handle sticking out of the waves like a lifebuoy. The voice was reprimanding him.

'I thought I told you to fetch Mrs Houghton down for lunch, Cridge! The others have finished and gone to their rooms and I'm afraid we can't keep the stew a minute longer!'

'I'm so sorry, Mrs Routledge!' (The pounding noise had stopped and there was silence. Cridge looked round him hopelessly at Mrs Houghton's room with Johnny and Melinda disappeared into thin air, and Mrs Houghton smiling apologetically at Mrs Routledge. He bowed his head and shuffled to what was now very clearly a door, hard and sticky to his touch.) 'I got rather carried away! But I'm not much of a luncher! Don't worry about me!'

Mrs Routledge still stood with her arms folded over her stomach. She wondered what Cridge had been doing up here all this time, and it crossed her mind that Mrs Houghton might be trying to take him on as a servant. Her air of suspicion deepened.

'I would like to invite you to a small party I'm giving here in the hotel,' she said nevertheless, for it was important to her that Mrs Houghton should come to it. 'To meet Mr Rathbone – our proprietor, you know. I do hope you're free?'

Mrs Houghton packed away her manuscript. She looked preoccupied and tired after the scene, and her tone was vague when she answered.

'I'd simply love to. How very kind. About six-thirty tomorrow?'

'And any relatives of yours if you'd care to,' Mrs Routledge added in spite of herself. 'Mr Rathbone is being knighted today, you know. I had no idea, but Miss Briggs pointed it out to me in the papers. So modest, the dear man made no mention of it at all!'

'I'll see. They may have gone away for a little breath of air in the country.'

'Of course.'

'Thank you anyway.'

Mrs Routledge realized she was being elbowed out of the room. Mrs Houghton was taking fresh paper and now she inserted a page in the typewriter and sat down in front of it. To show her respect, Mrs Routledge tiptoed noisily out into the corridor and down the stairs to the hall. She looked embarrassed as she went: Mr Poynter's afternoon snores were particularly loud today.

Mr Poynter was in his El Dorado. The City was as beautiful and as calm as ever, but he could see, since his morning visit and the interruption of lunch, that trouble was brewing underneath: a battalion of soldiers had just finished pushing the walls of the ghetto back into place – from the blood and trampled roses in the streets he could see it had been a violent night – and the workers who stood back respectfully from his car as he passed looked pale and preoccupied. He also noticed a strange whining sound, and wondered at first if it came from his own ear. Repeated proddings proved it did not, and he leaned forward to tap the chauffeur's shoulder and inquire whether the main transmitter of the City – in the glass radio station where he made his most important pronouncements – had somehow gone haywire and was producing this disturbing noise. The chauffeur shook his head in answer to the question.

'No one here has had any sleep with the whine going on, sir. We think it's coming from underground, it might be voices, sir.'

'Voices?' Poynter wound down the window of the Rolls and stuck out his head. He saw that the blossom on the trees in the Central Park had gone, and shining red and green apples hung there in its place, and cursed the behaviour of time in dreams, where a carefully laid plan could be disrupted just like that by a jump in season or time of day. Serious rebellions might have been under way and he too late on the scene to execute anything other than a mopping up operation. (Otherwise, he had to admire the bright autumn of his City. Tints from the calendar he and Mrs Poynter had ordered every year and hung over the mantelpiece at home shone deep russet and red in the park and tree-lined boulevards. The regulated nip in the air gave him a sudden sense of well-being.)

'They don't sound like voices to me,' he went on, and as soon as he had said this recognized the whine as just that: subterranean sirens, chained in dungeons beneath the foundations of the City, giving voice to their despair and grief in a language as familiar as echoes from the cradle and as impossible to understand. He wound the window back up again with a snap.

'Where are those women who were found in my Residence?' he asked sharply. 'They've been dealt with presumably?'

'They're in the dungeons,' the chauffeur confirmed his worst suspicions. 'Awaiting your pleasure, sir.'

Mr Poynter sat back and considered. There was no doubt the high wail was remarkably similar to the revolting sounds Miss Scranton had let out at the end of lunch. And as he approached HQ, and the great courtyard which formed an impenetrable ceiling to the prisons below, the noise grew louder. He dreaded the thought of seeing Miss Scranton again – naked, and probably disease-ridden by now – and the thought flashed through his mind to give an order to the firing squad and put an end to it. Then he reflected that this way of dealing with the problem would offend Mrs Houghton's concepts of moderation, and cancelled the thought. He had decided to marry Mrs Houghton in the City today, to prevent her from escaping him again, and a mass execution on one's wedding day was hardly to be tolerated. He stepped stiffly out of the car on arrival at the marble and gilt portals of HQ and stood to attention before his troops.

The Salute went as usual, but Mr Poynter could see that all was not well with the men. He braced himself after the twenty-one cannon shots had temporarily erased the maddening whine, and went over to his second-in-command. Today he forgot to take pleasure in the wheat-yellow hair of the men, and the blue eyes that lay like a stripe on a medal before him. He spoke tersely, the ostrich feather in his helmet moving up and down with slow deliberation as he made his announcement.

'I am getting married today, Struthers. Please see that the ceremonial marquee is erected in the Central Park and inform the caterers. Also, conduct me instantly with a guard to the dungeons. The problem of these women must be solved forthwith.'

Struthers, an indispensable part of Mr Poynter's machine, bowed low.

'And by the way, have you seen my fiancée?' The Commandant-in-Chief went on. He concealed his nervousness at a possible negative reply by clicking his heels together and putting his hand to his sword. Immediately the army in the courtyard in front of him clicked their heels in unison and bright blades flashed in the air. The deafening roar subsided, and Struthers was saying:

'She is waiting in your Residence, sir. May I be the first to congratulate you, sir. We felt something was afoot, as her ladyship ordered a magnificent gown from the couturier only this morning.'

Poynter suppressed a smile of triumph. If Mrs Houghton was hard to get in the Westringham, here she was malleable, to say the least. He was glad, too, that she had assumed a title fitting to her new station in life. He nodded to his bodyguard – Swiss men, not one of them under six and a half feet – who had appeared at his side, and made for the door leading to the dungeons. Once this unpleasant task was over, he was sure nothing but happiness lay ahead. There had evidently been unrest – the state of the ghetto and the expressions of the men testified to that – but he would put an end to the whine (he was not yet quite sure how he would do this), and serenity and order would be restored. The low door swung open and he went down the damp, evil-smelling steps. Struthers walked beside him, a body of giants bringing up the rear.

'What measures have you taken so far, Struthers?' The whine grew unbearably loud, and Mr Poynter noticed that he was beginning to experience the sensations of guilt normally associated with a long night in the moving streets. He glanced covertly at his companion, and saw that Struthers too wore an expression of deep embarrassment and shame.

'So this is what the men have been suffering,' Poynter said quietly before Struthers could reply. 'Subversive warfare. They're well nigh exhausted by their guilt by now, I suppose?' Struthers assented mutely. They came to the iron door of the largest dungeon and he produced a key, sliding it into the rusty keyhole

83

with one hand and covering his right ear against the noise with the other. Poynter looked behind him and saw that even his bodyguard had grown pale, several of the men actually shaking and the tallest and strongest leaning against the oozing wall as if he wouldn't be able to stand the sound a minute longer. As leader, Poynter refrained from blocking his ears, but his heart was pounding and his throat dry. Memories of the late Mrs Poynter's frequent attacks of helpless sobbing returned to him. Her inexplicable grief and his own feelings of anger and impotence in the face of it. He realized then that he had constructed his City precisely in order to be removed from this sound for ever; and the rage which swept over him at finding it multiplied under his very headquarters gave him the strength to look in at the dungeon with an appearance of steely resolution. Struthers, shouting over the intolerable keening, was punctiliously giving his chief details of the measures taken against the women in his absence.

'We didn't want to act without instructions,' he shouted. 'But the men were coming down here at first to try and comfort them and stop the noise and we administered oral contraceptives. I hope that meets with your approval, sir?'

Poynter shuddered at the thought of the contamination of his perfect race which would result from the men coupling with these Amazons. He nodded gratefully. 'You've stopped the soldiers, I trust?' he asked Struthers, at the same time scanning the awful contents of the dungeon with a wary eye. The women looked as filthy, desperate and matted as he had expected; some were chained to the black walls, others lay on straw and thrashed their legs slowly as they keened. When they saw the men at the door the hubbub rose in volume, and Poynter heard the terrified steps of half his bodyguard as they ran back to the stairs and open air.

'No, it didn't do any good,' Struthers bellowed. 'They wouldn't stop it for anything. What are your instructions, sir?'

Poynter was silent while his mind raced. He thought of gas, starvation and solitary confinement; and at each solution he imagined the horrified response of his bride-to-be. There were too many of them to contemplate release: the idea of an attack on the City walls at night from this tribe was hardly enjoyable. He stalled,

84

while the almost comprehensible moaning rose and fell about him like waves in some human Sargasso sea.

'Gas?' said Struthers hopefully. Poynter shook his head. Then a figure detached itself from the thick crowd of women in the gloom at the far end of the dungeon and darted towards him, a bruised, sand-encrusted arm came down on his before the bodyguard could intervene.

'Mr Poynter!'

Of course: Miss Scranton. Poynter's stomach heaved at the sight of the schoolmistress, naked again and looking up at him with the adoration he had suddenly noticed at the end of lunch earlier that day. Her eyes shone through a bushy fringe of hair, she was babbling something; Poynter pulled off the guard and stooped to listen. He thought he could make out the words. He would conquer his nausea. He put on a benevolent expression, and a murmur of surprise came from Struthers and his men behind him.

'I can stop them!'

This was what Miss Scranton was saying! Mr Poynter could hardly believe it. He swore to himself that he would be kinder to her in future, cut out the snubs which had hitherto greeted every one of her remarks at mealtimes in the Westringham. He took her hand and squeezed it.

'How, my dear? How?'

'I don't want to be here!' Miss Scranton's eyes filled with tears and Mr Poynter recoiled. But she kept a tight grip on his arm.

'I don't belong with these women! It was all the most awful mistake! Let me go, Mr Poynter, and I'll make sure they're quiet. They think I'm their emissary, you see.'

Poynter thought quickly. Miss Scranton's suggestion sounded a reasonable one.

'Let me see you quieten them,' he said. Struthers muttered approval at his cunning and he smiled to himself. Not for nothing was Poynter Commandant-in-Chief of the beautiful City.

Miss Scranton turned to face the Amazons and held up a hand. A low, inarticulate stream of sound came out of her mouth. The whine faltered; and stopped. There was silence. A woman's leg could be heard moving in the straw.

'You see, Mr Poynter? I told them they would be released in twenty-four hours if they were quiet all that time. It's up to you of course, what you do then.'

'My dear Miss Scranton, I really can't thank you enough. Struthers, find a blanket for Miss Scranton and take her to H Q. She may have a bath and order any delicacy she wishes to eat. Then she is to be set free.'

'Free?' Miss Scranton sounded distressed at the thought.

But by now Mr Poynter was halfway down the passage and going fast in case the tone of complaint should come into her voice again. He reached the stairs, anxious for a glimpse of Mrs Houghton in her magnificent gown, for a leisurely discussion in his residence of the wedding later in the afternoon.

'Freedom of the City I mean,' he called back over his shoulder.

'Struthers, please make sure Miss Scranton is awarded the freedom of the City.'

'Yes sir,' Struthers said.

Poynter climbed into his white Rolls and cruised through the streets to his residence. He thought he could detect symptoms of instantaneous relief on the features of his subjects: the workers, out for their factory break, were strolling and laughing; the exiled dictators saluted him with pleasure and gratitude rather than envy from their lawns. As he went up the grand boulevard that culminated in his fine white house, he saw a familiar figure – small and scurrying modestly across the road to avoid the slowing of his car, but unmistakable, and he let out a low grunt of astonishment.

'Isn't that the Queen?' he demanded of his chauffeur.

The man inclined his head.

'Her Majesty arrived a short time ago and is living in the turreted house opposite yours, sir. If I may say so, sir, I would like to congratulate you on solving the woman problem here in the City. How long will they be quiet for sir?'

'There's a new rule,' Poynter snapped. 'The future tense is now banned in the City. It will be used only on ceremonial occasions, by myself.'

'Yes sir.'

The Rolls drew up outside Mr Poynter's residence. At the end of the archway of sprinklers, on the gleaming steps, Mrs Houghton stood in a white and gold gown that took Mr Poynter's breath away. He almost fell out of the car in his eagerness to greet her. And he reflected, as he went through the glittering drops of water, that it would be nice for the future Mrs Poynter to have the Queen living so very close.

While the dreams of the residents of the Westringham Hotel tangled and unfolded, binding their victims together in terrible juxtapositions and snapping them apart just at the moment when they seemed most inextricably interwoven, there began to creep out of the doors and into the streets and over the countryside the faint, invisible strands of these dreams, which came down in ghostly loops over the innocent and the unsuspecting and the corrupt alike. Stockbrokers and barristers wandered half the day in Mr Poynter's City, eyes glazed and expressions abstracted as they passed under Grecian porticoes and into buildings of glass as fine and shimmering as the droplets of water from Mr Poynter's sprinkler. Housewives and women at desks in offices saw suddenly long beaches, and a flat warm sea, and felt sand encrusted on their wrists and their legs heavy. Royalty breathed out from newspapers and magazines, enveloping and protecting and carrying their prey to an unchanging and benevolent world. Already Mr Rathbone, pulled in as it were from the right of the Westringham – which was spinning now at increasing speed, like a bobbin out of control, the material beneath the needle torn and rumpled – stumbled through his impossible mixture of dream and reality. To the left, the filaments spread in many directions – and the first to be caught, to suffer the illusions and fight for the dreams which were awakened in him, was a young man, no longer so young perhaps, by the name of Marcus Tapp.

Marcus Tapp was a waiter at the White Horses Hotel, Frinton-on-Sea. At lunchtime on this momentous day he walked into the dining-room holding an oblong plate on which lay fried plaice, chips, a slice of lemon and a large lettuce leaf which looked as if something was hiding under it although in fact its function was to conceal the foodless portion of the plate. He set this collection down before the solitary, out-of-season guest and went over to the window to look out at the sea. The White Horses had a curved window in the dining-room, and cornered more of the sea than the other hotels on the front: whichever way you looked the grey pencilled waves seemed to run parallel with you; and this was generally considered the triumph of the architect, an ambitious Lutyens' school man at the turn of the century, that he had marshalled the sea to run according to his plan. Today, because low tide coincided with lunchtime (and even this architect had found himself unable to control the tides), the view from the window was a desolate one. Plastic and cardboard debris littered the beach. An old man and a boy, in the far distance where the sea would have been visible if the clouds had not come down in the intervening stretch and obscured it, were digging for lugworms. The rows of bathing huts, awkward on their slender wooden legs, looked like an abandoned shanty town, left suddenly by the worker inhabitants once the splendid buildings on the Front were completed – or a necropolis, unvisited and unkempt. There was the promise of rain in the sky. While the guest ate slowly and suspiciously at the table behind him, Marcus Tapp folded his arms over his tails and permitted himself a heavy sigh.

Marcus Tapp had fallen far. In the heady days of '68 he had been a professional revolutionary, and this role had sustained him for several years afterwards. He was young, but had a shock of white hair, which lent weight to his pronouncements – most of these were cryptic, consisting as they did of the barking out of strings of initials representing the various political groups with which he was involved or at war. He had fought, marched and gone underground. Rich, guilty girls had made their parents' houses and their own incomes available to him: he had 'occupied' stately homes up and down the country, 'liberated' five-course dinners in famous restaurants, and 'ripped off' books he needed from leading bookshops in London. As the revolutionary fervour sagged, and publishers, rather than offer him handsome advances for his explanation of his times and the times to come, were mysteriously 'tied up' when he called, Marcus toyed briefly with mysticism and acid rock. But he was too late to make anything of these phenomena. And not really suited to them either: he liked to impose order, to make a conscious collective instead of plunging into the collective unconscious; there weren't enough initials in the Universe; as far as music was concerned he was unfortunately tone deaf. A kind and impoverished aunt in Gloucester replaced his guilty, noble supporters, and he was reduced to expounding his views on the smashing of capitalism to her in a small front room where the cat snuffled and the gas fire gave him a headache. Occasionally friends sent drugs through the post – cut into the spines of books usually, Marcus's aunt had valiantly tried to read a mutilated copy of *The Mayor of Caster-bridge* which had arrived in this way – but after a while, with rising prices and no feedback from Marcus, even this stopped. The aunt died, showing the feeble malice for which her nephew had so often berated her (she was petit bourgeois, he told her, Poujadist, she was the enemy of the revolution) by leaving her remaining five hundred pounds to a cats' home. Marcus took a job as a waiter, for all that was left to him was to feel his identity in peril, he had read Sartre on waiters and hoped to re-emerge when the time was ripe with a host of ideological anecdotes; Frinton offered the best wages and an attic room overlooking the sea. In the evenings he read Engels and Lacan and Gramsci and Adorno and Deutscher's *Trotsky* and thought of his family, one of the oldest banking families in England and by no means un-sympathetic to his views. They would not give him any money, however, for the turning of these views into reality, and as a result he had been cut off from them for some time. He thought of the delicious nursery food of his childhood while the chef at the White Horses smeared coloured breadcrumbs on to the deep-frozen fish, and for each bout of bourgeois individualism he punished himself late at night in his tiny room. Guests on the floor below, comfortable with their Neville Shute and H. E. Bates, became anxious at the sound of Guevara and Mao read loudly at the starless sky and Marcus was reprimanded by the proprietor for his strange habits. He had taken to pacing the Front now in his time off and reciting his favourite passages. The few all-the-year-round inhabitants of Frinton found him a familiar, reassuring figure as he strode, always in his tails and always at high tide, along the ramp. Sometimes children ran behind him with shrimping nets like small disciples. Once or twice, in the season, he was photographed as he went by a curious tourist.

The guest in the hotel dining-room today was a middle-aged woman who resembled the mother of Marcus's ex-girl-friend. Marcus's ex-girl-friend, Moira, had left him three years ago after joining a feminist group at his instigation, and since then he had had no desire for a close relationship with a woman. He missed her all the same, when he lay on his narrow bed and contemplated the blank years ahead before the revolution, and on one occasion he had telephoned her from the staff paybox to say he wished she would come back to him. She had told him she would only do this when he was reconstructed, and he had rung off sadly, for women played little part in his idea of socialism. He had hoped to find Moira a perfect companion both for his revolutionary activities – she was strong and agile and could run with an illegal radio transmitter from a squat faster than the fuzz could catch her – and for his moments of leisure, when she would roll joints (which she provided with the money from secretarial work) in the flat she paid for and kept clean. It hadn't worked out like that, Moira had begun to insist on shared housework, although she went on paying the rent without complaining for a time, and things had reached a point between them where she actually contradicted him on points of theory and looked sulky when he objected to this. Despite his bitterness at her change of heart, Marcus was disturbed at the close resemblance of the woman eating the fish he had served her: Moira's mother, unlike Moira, had agreed with his views on the most satisfactory role for her daughter, and once had come round to the flat and spent several hours trying to persuade her that she was lucky to have Marcus at all. He left the window and went with his waiter's walk over to the table. The woman was sitting gloomily in front of her empty plate and he saw she had even eaten the lettuce leaf, which was a rare thing for guests to do, counted on not to happen in fact, with the same leaf garnishing a succession of plates. He concluded she was not used to eating in restaurants, and looked at her more closely. The woman glanced up at him, but did not smile.

The guest looked almost like an intellectual, Marcus decided.

She had taken no exercise since arriving that morning, but had been seen in the hall poring over the tide tables, as if information about the movement of the sea was more important and edifying than the sight of the sea itself. She wore thin shoes, and there was no sign (this reported by the chambermaid) of wellington boots or plimsolls in her room. There were plenty of books there though (the chambermaid had not said which) and Marcus, stirred by memories of Moira and happy days with her and her mother in a cottage in the south of Devon, felt like asking her what she had come here for. He found himself wondering if she were by some long arm of chance a Trotskyist, but this seemed unlikely. He hovered by her chair, and said in a doleful voice:

'Would Madam care for a sweet?'

The woman turned, for Marcus was pointing at the sweet trolley, and considered for a moment the greying artificial cream on the trifle and the eruptions of chocolate on the tray beneath it. She shook her head.

'Coffee?'

'Please. Black.' Her voice was firm but breathy, encouraging to Marcus, who had heard only the soft hiss of refined talk since his arrival in the dining-room of the White Horses at Frinton. He tried to imagine how to formulate his questions: nothing too direct, as this would not befit a waiter; not too servile, as she might be put off answering him except in the vaguest way. He remembered the low, rapid tone of the mutual criticism sessions of his past, and plunged into a question without further ado. The woman gazed at him, startled, as he said:

'If it might not be too impertinent to inquire, what are the motives for the visit?'

'My dear man!' The woman seemed quite amused. 'D'you mean to say you've noticed nothing?'

Marcus's heart began to beat faster. It seemed impossible that things could be moving again in the world beyond his attic room. He had given up the stagnant society, with its Common Market preoccupations and obsession with inflation long ago, but it was true he had stopped reading *Le Monde* some months back and the woman might know something he didn't. He leered at her in his surprise, and as a response she waved an arm vigorously at the great curved window that lay before them.

'Do you know how long the tide has been out? It's increased!'

'The tide?' Marcus still smiled, but now with condescension. The woman was clearly a crank, and if he allowed her to talk his afternoon reciting on the Front would be gone. He made a surreptitious movement in the direction of the kitchens, the empty plate expertly balanced on his forearm and a napkin fluttering from his hand.

'It's been low tide for twenty-four hours now. I'm astonished you haven't noticed.' (The woman looked quite severe now, and no longer resembled Moira's mother.) 'The manager here is most concerned about the phenomenon, I can assure you. Don't you ever look out of the window?'

Marcus went to the curved expanse of plate glass and stood there a moment. He recollected that yesterday he had particularly looked forward to his walk today because the water would be right up by 2 p.m. and the soothing sound of the waves helped him in his declamations. And there was no sign of it coming in! Its absence throughout the last revolution of the sun would account for the rubbish piled up on the beach. It seemed further away than ever, if possible. He began to believe the strange guest, and turned back to her, agitated. She must be a scientist, a marine biologist of some kind. She would be able to explain it all to him. He felt something exciting was about to happen, and it would be intolerable to be left out of it all, a seedy waiter on the top floor of the White Horses while the world went into apocalypse round him.

The woman's chair was empty. Even her scrumpled-up napkin on the floor by the chair looked frightening and significant. Marcus ran to the service stairs and up into the reception hall. She was there, conferring with the manager; and he waited impatiently for the whispered conference to be over so that he could ask what the meaning of all this could be. But when she had finished speaking, she brushed past him and went through the swing doors out on to the windy promenade. She gazed at the receded sea through binoculars. Shivering with cold and anticipation Marcus stood at her side, his texts forgotten and a premonition of violent times to come running like electric current through his frame.

A gloomy evening settled in over the Westringham Hotel. Mr Poynter lay in bed waiting for the summons to Mrs Routledge's cold Wednesday supper; and from where he lay, framed by the cheap curtains at the window, the sky appeared thick and white, like a wad of cottonwool about to come down on him, blocking his ears and eyes and coming finally to his mouth and nostrils so that he would sleep forever under it. He was dozing, and as the sky gathered at the windowpane, made an ominous wall against the glass (as if Mr Poynter and his room had become detached from Earth and were floating, fragile, in an expanse of heavy cloud, soon to be permeated, absorbed, forgotten), he wandered half within the Westringham and half beneath the blue dome of his immortal City. Bright rosebuds and lawns as green as colour catalogues alternated with his bedroom furniture, the single armchair and its viscous cover, the cracked, tiny basin just to the right of his head when he sat up. A stately portico came and went beside the imitation walnut wardrobe, like a magic pillar of white fire. In the dusty corner by the door his soldiers sometimes stood, scarlet arms glowing and fading again by the golf club he had bought at Lost Property to impress Mrs Routledge before booking into the hotel. He saw the outer wall of the City where the narrow partition with Room 22, Miss Scranton's, should have been: castellated, clean slabs of Portland stone washed down twice a day; a tangle of barbed wire on top; the look-out boxes with their sweeping lights and a machine gun sticking out like the paw of a hunting dog at the undulating countryside beyond. He inhaled, and smelt the hawthorn fragrance of his youth, the ripe blackberries that grew all the year round in the preserved landscape of this dream. Then the partition (no cornice, no picture rail even, no illusion to mask the fact that Mrs Routledge had carved two rooms out of one, and Miss Scranton lay embarrassingly the other side of two inches of hardboard and bobbly wall-paper) swam once more before Mr Poynter's eyes. He heard his name spoken, then it was cried. He sat up and stared anxiously at the flimsy barrier. Miss Scranton was calling him. She sobbed as she uttered his name. She seemed to expect no answer. She was evoking him. Mr Poynter's blood froze and he sat bolt upright, his eyes screwed shut in an effort to remember the events of the afternoon, to block out this terrifying and yet somehow gratifying sound.

The wedding had gone without a hitch. After the unpleasant visit to the dungeons, and an escape from Miss Scranton – who had been led away by Struthers with promises of fine clothes and a romantic meeting later with her hero – Poynter had bathed and changed in the most stately suite at HQ and made his way to the Residence and the waiting bride. He was in tails, which he recognized with a slight pang of guilt as being the same as those he had hired so many years ago for his first wedding to Mrs Poynter, and there was a large pink carnation in his buttonhole. This memory was a replay for Poynter, who had realized on waking that he should not have been so hasty to reach Mrs Houghton without first preparing himself as a groom: there had been no time for a crowd in wedding mood: and he hoped to avoid having to see Her Majesty the Queen, whose presence might spoil this important day. He had smiled, and waved graciously. Mrs Houghton was there in the gold and white gown when he arrived, and a select band of guests had assembled in the room he had never used with Mrs Poynter, although they had designed it together to remind themselves of their happy past – a kind of Giant Front Room, where the piano and the aspidistras and the wireless they had listened to Churchill's speeches on were exactly duplicated but at least three times their original size. (He saw, on going into this room with Mrs Houghton, that she shrank from it rather, and he hissed a promise in her ear that she should have carte blanche to invite the most fashionable interior decorator in the City to do it up: it was hardly the place where Lady Kitty Carson could be repaid for her hospitality.) There were flowers everywhere, and the grateful Mr Poynter saw that his bride had had a hand in these – a harp made entirely of sweet peas and roses, gladioli forming arrangements of drawn swords on the vast brown walls, sweet little nosegays carried by the bridesmaids. Mrs Houghton herself held a bouquet of lilies, and was surrounded by a contingent of old nannies and page boys dressed in tartan kilts. There were even a few dogs about – and at first Mr Poynter frowned at this, no dogs were allowed to foul his City – but his bride murmured that her cousins down from Scotland and up from Wiltshire could hardly be expected to leave their Labradors behind and Mr Poynter melted into consent. His heart was bursting with happiness. It was a real country wedding, he could see that – on the lawn outside a point-to-point was taking place, with more young cousins of Mrs Houghton's soaring over hurdles on their little black mounts, and a tent where tenant farmers and old retainers were drinking tea and champagne and eating egg sandwiches. He bent down awkwardly and patted one of the strange dogs, and laughed with the others when it snarled at him in return. A young reporter, cheeks ruddy from country living, eyes nervous and overawed by having to approach the Leader, came up to him and asked where they intended to honeymoon, and here Mrs Houghton broke in and said, 'The Country, after all what could be nicer than that?' And Mr Poynter agreed, although he had never been outside the walls of his City. He wondered if the model villages and farms and ancient monuments, planned as they were to afford him the best possible view from his balcony, might not be too close together if they were actually visited, so that there would be little privacy for a honeymoon couple, but Mrs Houghton seemed to be able to read his mind and reassured him on this point as well. 'I've looked out there, darling, and there are the most divine walks. Not a soul for miles!' Although his heart sank slightly, for Mr Poynter had been brought up in a town and was afraid of cows, he gave his happy nod again. The music from the private chapel was calling them. Mrs Houghton looked demure and went to seek out an aged, kilted man who would 'give her away', her father being long dead, and Mr Poynter braced himself for the coming ceremony. The Front Room emptied as the guests went over the sward to the plain little church Mr Poynter had constructed there in the days of his frequent visits to the ghetto; the Swiss Bodyguard stood saluting by the door, and he went, head high, to wed the woman of his choice.

At this point in Mr Poynter's memory of the dream, the wailing from the next room grew louder and Miss Scranton's fist began to pound against the wall. Poynter opened his eyes and his mouth and shouted back.

'Will you stop that accursed noise please? It really is becoming impossible in here to concentrate at all!'

'But I need you! I'm at HQ, I was told to wait here!'

Miss Scranton sounded pathetic and desperate, and for a moment Mr Poynter struggled with his conscience. Perhaps he had allowed her to get away with the idea that he would reward her with his love after she had stopped the Amazons from bringing chaos and unrest to his City. But surely not? She must have seen, this morning at tea, how immediately drawn to Mrs Houghton he had been: there was no comparison between the two women whatever. In a last tenuous attempt at reality Mr Poynter reminded himself sternly that it was out of the question for Miss Scranton to be at his HQ. She was in Room 22 and that was all there was to it. But she sounded convinced enough; and it crossed his mind that if she went on making this din Mrs Houghton might overhear and be cold to him at supper. He crept out of bed and went at an unusual speed to the thin greasy partition, put his cupped mouth up against the hard wallpaper so that the bobbles (it was thus designed to conceal cracks and bad workmanship beneath) pressed on his lips like popcorn.

'Please Miss Scranton! I'll come and see you in a moment if you'll just be good enough to keep quiet!'

There was a silence, in which Mr Poynter thought he could hear the hum of Mrs Houghton's typewriter down the passage. Thank goodness for that! But once they had settled down to married life he had no intention of letting his wife pursue her career as a novelist. She would have too many duties to attend to. He made a mental note to be firm about this after the country honeymoon.

'Are you really coming?' Miss Scranton said in a low whine that set Mr Poynter's teeth on edge. He rubbed at his chafed lips and whispered hoarsely back:

'Do I ever break my word? Just pipe down and I will come!'

Now the silence seemed more certain. Mr Poynter went back to bed and closed his eyes again. He remembered the ceremony, with the thrilling moment when Mrs Houghton had said I do, and the kiss at the end of the service. The music played loudly and they went out on the lawn, where Mrs Houghton threw her bouquet and it was caught by an eager bridesmaid. Then, as he remembered, his brows went together in a frown and his eyes snapped open again. Of course – there had been a mistake in the dream at that point – the first Mrs Poynter had appeared at the french windows of the Blue Room and a shriek had gone up from the celebrating guests. She had been naked, and with matted hair like the Amazons. She was carrying a spear, and it was pointed at Mr Poynter's heart. He thought he could see hordes of naked women behind her. He had woken in a sweat, but not before seeing the look on his bride's face. The bewilderment, the disappointment! And then the contempt! The word bigamist had gone round the sward, hissed in the tent and fallen at the hurdles, retainers had poured out to hurl abuse at him, young innocent country cousins run to hide in the brushwood shelters they had erected for the afternoon's sport. Poynter had made for the french windows. But his legs folded under him, and there was laughter. When he was properly awake – yes, there was the empty aspirin packet – he remembered swallowing three of them, and for him this was unprecedentedly rash. How would he make things right with Mrs Houghton later this evening? How could he prove, without vulgarly producing his wife's death certificate, that Mrs Poynter had been gone twenty years and had only survived in his dreams until he met the woman he had always been looking for? He lay thinking, eyes resolutely wide open. There was still silence from the next room, but he decided to go and visit Miss Scranton before she started to raise hell again. It would hardly help matters at supper if Miss Scranton presented herself as yet another candidate for his affections. Wearily, Poynter pulled his dressing gown over his sunken shoulders and went out into the corridor of the Westringham Hotel.

Jeannette Scranton, who had suffered from remorse since child-hood – her father had had no desire to commit incest with her, her mother had compensated for this lack of interest by climbing frequently into her bed, Jeannette's first remorse stemmed from having been the unwilling disrupter of their marriage (and her successive bouts of remorse, too, had come from finding herself insufficiently inspiring to God for Him to fill her with religious zeal, uncharismatic with her pupils so that they had no wish to learn anything at all) – suffered, as she lay in a half-waking state in her bed in Room 22, from one of the worst attacks she had known for a long time. She had betrayed her friends. She had lied to them, promising freedom in return for their silence, when she knew very well there was not and never could be a comfortable place for them within the walls of Mr Poynter's City. She had done this to gain the affections of Mr Poynter. Mr Poynter was not only not interested in her, but passionately in love with Mrs Houghton; and she felt, added to her existing remorse, a deep throb of the remorse for the future when she was bound to try and disrupt their relationship, inject another few drops of misery into a world which could well do without it. Why was she like this? How could it be that she had heard herself crying out for Mr Poynter? She was making the very sound of which he had so rightly complained in the dungeons: she knew he was only in-terested in that sound as far as finding a suitable method of stopping it; yet (and it was horrifying to think that even the first Mrs Poynter, after her long years of submission, had joined the Amazons and Jeannette was incapable of it) she was calling out for him as Judas had vainly called on the name of Christ after the act of treachery. For Jeannette had not only sold her sisters into slavery for the faint promise of a special position in Mr Poynter's world, she had brought about the downfall of Mr Poynter on his most glorious day. Scorned, hearing the news of the wedding from the cheering crowds outside the windows of the neat little guest house to which she had been politely removed by Struthers and an attendant retinue of lady's maids and footmen, she had taken advantage of her freedom of the City to release the furious women and unleash them on her unsuspecting host. Led by the first Mrs Poynter, they had stormed down the wide streets and boulevards and up the great avenue to the Residence. The crowds had fallen back in fear, and the soldiers had turned tail and run back to barracks, where they had locked themselves in. The women had seized arms – and this Jeannette had not foreseen – from the artillery wing of HQ; they had carbines and muskets and pistols and machine guns, and cartridge belts that thumped against their naked flanks as they marched. After what seemed only a moment, but it could have been more (Jeannette was used to this disturbing sense of flying and stopping time in her dreams), she heard the sound of gunshots and the quick sharp rattle of the machine guns, which sounded from the window of the house where she stood, like an angrier, more confident version of the incomprehensible language with which they had communicated in the dungeons. A blue haze rose into the sky above the battle-fields of Mr Poynter's wedding. It was then, still dozing, remembering herself in the house he had so kindly presented to her – and in a beautiful shot silk dress, which suited her, she felt, as nothing had before – that she cried out for him. She banged on the partition wall, to obliterate the sound of the guns. The view of Mr Poynter's City faded, and she saw the thin hump of her body beneath the bedclothes. Cridge, back from the shops with his store of cocktail food and lacy mats, trudged past on his way up to hand these trophies to Mrs Routledge. Cecilia Houghton's typewriter could be heard to falter and then to start blithely up again. Miss Briggs called out once, and then was silent. Mr Poynter's voice came through the wall and Jeannette sat up, her blood freezing in her veins. He would come to her! If she was quiet! She sank down in the bed, fists clenched at her side in an attempt at self-control and only her eyes, wild as those of the women she had betrayed and falsely liberated, showing above the thin sheet.

Mr Poynter came in and sat down on the end of Jeannette Scranton's bed. He was shaking badly, she saw, but it was difficult to believe she wasn't dreaming, so near and yet so immeasurably far did Mr Poynter seem, tangible and yet impossible to touch. He was looking at her, but she could not meet his gaze (for who has ever looked into the eyes of another in a dream?); instead she stared at the contents of her room as if seeing them for the first time in her life. Her past suddenly became clear to her. The photograph of her mother in the heart-shaped frame showed an alien face with a hint of a moustache about the lips, a thin, bent nose that looked as if it had been stuck on to express disapproval at the way the world was made. The stuffed salmon, caught by Jeannette's father just before the outbreak of the First World War – in order to try and interest him she had shown enthusiasm in fishing and he had bequeathed it to her in his will: it lay as heavy on her as the remorse she had always felt for him – disintegrated before her eyes to scales and stuffing and a gaping mouth amongst the dead ferns in the box. Her clothes – a pile of woollies and a sensible grey skirt folded neatly on the chest of drawers, could never have belonged to her. In her ecstasy at Mr Poynter's presence, Jeannette felt her identity disintegrate and a new one come to life. She moulded herself to suit him, and felt her limbs beneath the sheets grow full and round, a youthful blush creep to her cheeks. She looked at him at last, and smiled. But it was so hard to think that he was really there!

'Miss Scranton.'

Mr Poynter's voice trembled. Jeannette saw them in a country cottage and she waking early to prepare a good breakfast. He was pitifully thin and uncared for. 'Miss Scranton, I must ask you to join in an experiment with me.'

Jeannette's eyelashes fluttered – of their own accord; she had the delightful feeling of being quite out of control of her actions. She strengthened her smile. Outside, Cridge went grumbling past on his way down from Mrs Routledge, and she remembered with some pleasure that tonight he would not be in the dining-room. Cridge took up too much of Mr Poynter's time.

'What experiment?' She sounded arch, she knew, but he seemed serious. She cursed the sound of Mrs Houghton's type-writer down the passage at a moment like this.

'We must try and dream together. I feel we have been at cross purposes too long. Too concerned with our own dreams, perhaps, and not enough with the dreams of others.'

As he spoke, Mr Poynter put his hand on Jeannette's foot under the blankets. A warm glow spread up her leg, but she lay still. A momentary revulsion seized her: when the time came she had expected a slightly more subtle approach.

'I will certainly dream with you,' she said in a soft voice nonetheless.

'We must try and change our dreams,' Mr Poynter went on in his solemn, almost frightening tone. 'I am in a very difficult position now, as you must know.'

So he had regrets already! Jeannette felt a surge of sympathy for the man. He found himself married to a professional woman, a woman who would be unable to devote herself to him as a wife should. How could she tell him that she forgave his mistakes, that for him to admit he was not always in the right would wipe out her remorse of a lifetime and bring fulfilment to them both? Then, for she was not stupid, she had passed out of Training College with flying colours, Jeannette remembered that his mistake was not as irrevocable as he thought.

'Your marriage to Mrs Houghton is null and void,' she said. She sat up, and leaned forward to within a few inches of the longed-for face. She did not dare touch it yet, however. 'Your first wife is after all still alive,' she went on, and instantly regretted this, for poor Mr Poynter's eyebrows shot up and he looked unbearably confused. 'But insane,' Jeannette added quickly. 'There will be no need for a divorce, even. She can be certified insane. And you –' she let out a trilling laugh '– are quite free to marry whom you choose.'

Everything seemed to happen very quickly after that, and Jeannette had the only too familiar symptoms of nightmare as Mr Poynter leapt at her, battered her head with his fists so that she was knocked into a misty version of his City, saw stars in the blue sky over his Residence, smelled the blood and carnage the

103

Amazons had created in the streets. He swore in hatred at her, and if at first she felt his violence as an expression of his love, enjoyed his superior strength even, as he forced her to the scene of the battle and demanded she remove the women, she soon kicked and struggled at his impossible demand.

'There's nothing I can do about it now, Mr Poynter! They're out of my control. Ask your wife!'

Mr Poynter fell away from her at this. There was silence, apart from their panting and gasping, and a door down the passage opened quietly. Jeannette's left eyelid was bleeding, and as she tried to force it open she saw in one last horrifying glimpse, the Amazons shoot the little pink pills they had been given in the dungeons through the mouths of the machine guns into the air. Jeannette felt her womb contract and subside again. There were footsteps on the stairs leading to Mrs Routledge's room. Miss Briggs next door, in an unnaturally loud voice, said, 'Admit Mr Geoffrey Rathbone.' Several feet came to the door of Room 22 and it was flung open. Jeannette opened her eyes at last. Blood streamed down her face.

Mrs Routledge was standing in the doorway, and behind her was Mrs Houghton. They both gaped in disbelief at the scene before them. From the adjacent room came a loud thump and the sound of steel scraping from a scabbard.

'Rise, Sir Geoffrey!' Miss Briggs said. Deflected by this new disturbance Mrs Routledge turned and went heavily out over the creaking boards into the passage. Mrs Houghton stayed on, her arms folded across her stomach, a hard glint in her eyes as she contemplated Mr Poynter and Miss Scranton there.

Mrs Houghton had had a trying afternoon. Every scene with Johnny and Melinda had proved a failure – a visit to the Zoo (with Johnny proudly pointing out the territorial imperative of the male gorilla and Melinda, quiescent now after the violent years, clinging to Johnny's arm and laughingly agreeing) had resulted in a stand-up fight between the characters and another assault, by both of them this time, on the author herself. A large meal in a fashionable restaurant in Covent Garden, put in against her better instincts as a placatory scene before the departure of the couple for their married future in Dorset, had ended in Mrs Houghton's being ignominiously covered in avocado soup and potato salad just as she was launching on a description of the ageing pop stars and media men at the surrounding tables. She had truly begun to feel Johnny and Melinda beyond her control, and saw she must put an end to their dangerous antics at once if she was to survive herself; but the trouble here lay in the gospel of freedom and moderation she had always preached, and the dead wooden nature of the prose that always succeeded a decision to be more ruthless with them. If she simply sent them to Dorset, making sure they obeyed her outline to the letter, the readers would be bored and disappointed, after all the emotional up-heavals they had undergone, by their sudden capitulation to Mrs Houghton's will. It was a difficult moment, and although she had typed bravely on in the face of their increasingly murderous acts, she felt the onset of Block: a whitish blank in the head, like the beginning of a migraine, and not helped by the dull, low sky outside; a feverish impatience to be shot of the whole thing com-bined with a lingering love for her characters and a wild desire to change the shape of the plot in order to gain their approval. At the end of each paragraph she sat with her head in her hands at the table. Johnny now spoke only in American, which she recognized as a very bad sign indeed. Melinda's statements had become almost incomprehensible, and when she was supposed to be talking to her lover, discussing the meaning of the life they led together, she spoke instead in cryptic tones of the movement of the tides, the sway of the moon, and the day of victory, whatever that could possibly mean. Mrs Houghton had begun to doubt Melinda's sanity, and therefore, as she had always proudly believed Melinda to be a submerged fraction of herself, her own as well. She wondered if she should see a psychiatrist before completing the trilogy. The irritating and inexplicable noises from the other rooms in the Westringham Hotel only added to her despairing state.

As the afternoon wore on, and the effort to control Johnny and Melinda grew more and more exhausting, Cecilia Houghton found that each time she put her head in her hands at the typewriter she fell into a strange sleep. At first she half-welcomed the beautiful place that took shape as soon as her eyelids closed: the architecture of the broad streets, a soft blue sky that made her yearn for a holiday in the Mediterranean as soon as this wretched book was over, a fine park where fruit and blossom were magically intertwined on the branches of the trees. She liked the dress she was wearing, too – rather formal, perhaps, for a daytime stroll, but she could see the gold thread which danced in stars and moons on the soft white silk was real gold, and that hundreds of hours of work accounted for the simple look – she wondered if she were dreaming herself dead, and rewarded for her thankless life by wearing this splendid robe. She was an angel; and in the lovely garden towards which she seemed to be drawn every time she found herself in the City there was an admiring crowd, composed mainly of women in flowered hats, who applauded her and gave little gasps of admiration at every step she took. The garden was filled with water, and in the iridescent droplets which rose and fell around her she saw admiration and approval as well, as if the place had been constructed solely with her happiness in mind. The only drawback was that Mr Poynter was there – ridiculously got up in tails too small for him – and also that every time she saw him she had the unpleasant feeling of having been here with him

106

before. He stood beside her and from time to time eyed her possessively. Cecilia grew uncomfortable, and on several occasions forced herself awake; but there was something compelling about the dream and whenever she closed her eyes she was back in it again. She had a premonition she was about to get married, and as it was impossible to believe that even the most foolish dream would suggest Mr Poynter as the bridegroom, she allowed herself to remember her own wedding so long ago. Johnny and Melinda, abandoned in mid-sentence in a borrowed Ford Anglia on the way to Dorset, faded from her mind. Dozing, against a half-formed background of the chapel at Mr Poynter's residence and the swell of the wedding march as it floated out over the herbaceous borders, Cecilia rocked gently in her chair and summoned up memories of her poor husband and the joyful days before his fatal illness, which had been bravely borne. (She had commemorated him in a short novel, *On Second Thoughts*, and won a prize of one hundred guineas for the slow painful description of his last hours.) She saw herself and Mr Houghton at the altar, he already leaning heavily on a stick and a nurse discreetly tucked away at the back of the church, and heard his faint stumbling acceptance of the marriage tie. A soft smile spread over her features as she remembered the honeymoon, the hotel chosen for its proximity to one of the best hospitals in the south of England, the quiet walks along the top of the cliffs and the curious but sympathetic glances of the passing tourists as she struggled with the heavy wheelchair on the rough grass. Mr Houghton, even in the terminal stage, had continued to dictate his memoirs to a secretary at the bedside – the Houghtons had been an artistic pair, always poor but never swerving in their dedication to the Arts – unfortunately, because of a mistaken obsession with the secretary and certain damaging revelations about herself, she had had to suppress these, preferring to give an account of his life and work in *On Second Thoughts* than to suffer the humiliation of his posthumous publication. She remembered the little house in Eastbourne where they had lived, and the ground floor bedroom that rang with Mr Houghton's cough as she typed upstairs – and as the wedding reception at Mr Poynter's residence got under way and she found her hand on the knife,

107

the elegant cake yield its first slice at her touch, she saw her husband's last, unsuccessful operation (she insisted on witnessing this, the better to be able to describe it in her future works); and she felt again the sweet sadness of her early widowed years. A lump came into her throat. If her characters knew how she had suffered! When she lavished all her attention and compassion on them and they were thoroughly spoilt by it by now. If only she could suddenly insert an autobiographical passage into the narrative at this point, how ashamed of themselves they would be! But that was quite against the rules. She must continue to pander to their whims – perhaps, when this trilogy was done, she would indulge herself in a fuller and more heart-rending account of her life and sorrows than *On Second Thoughts* had dared to be.

While Mrs Houghton dreamed and reflected, Johnny and Melinda climbed out of the car on the edge of the motorway and stood in impotent fury beside ten lanes of westbound holiday traffic. Without thinking, the author had set them off on a Friday evening just when the jam was at its worst, and they had been crawling for over three hours now through the false countryside of the outer suburbs: golf courses so green and neat they looked as if the grass had been sprayed on them and then varnished down, ornamental lakes with a bitter poisonous sheen and dead weeds sticking out like fingers. The few birds sat in clumps in the bushes, and the sun appeared in short bursts between the bellies of the great planes as they came down to land a few miles away. Melinda walked up and down on the verge, her sense of claustrophobia at the impending incarceration with Johnny and the interminable line of cars expressed by her taut shoulders and downturned mouth. Johnny sat by the rear wheels of the Ford Anglia, smoking and gazing at her with the good-humoured contempt he knew she found insufferable. When she had turned, and was walking back towards him, he called out:

'We've made a mess of this one, ain't we? I thought you said you were going to get her while you were packing and she was giving you the last inner thoughts before setting off. What the hell happened?'

'She was too strong for me.' Melinda shot a glance of hatred at him and settled on the grass by the exhaust pipe. They had not spoken since leaving west London and she felt an angry relief that he had broken the silence, although she might attack him at any minute with one of the weapons reserved for Mrs Houghton in the back of the car – the air pistol (but he would soon grab that from her) or the ceremonial sword they had found in a glass case on their earlier visit to Miss Briggs's room. 'She made me sorry for her,' Melinda went on, for she knew that if she and Johnny were to survive they must remain united against their creator. 'It was awful!' She managed a wry laugh at this and the atmosphere improved slightly.

'She made you sorry for her? How the hell?'

'When she was giving me the thoughts. I knew they were hers really and she was just putting them into my mouth. All about happiness and grasp it while you can and how lucky I am to have you.' Melinda sighed. 'We are born and we suffer and we die,' she recited in a flat tone as Johnny stared at her in perplexity. 'She's had a bad time you know, Johnny. I'm beginning to wonder if she shouldn't be allowed to have her way after all.'

'Well I'm damned!' Johnny inserted a blade of grass between his teeth, frowned at the metallic taste and threw it under the car. 'One of the things that's wrong with our Mrs Houghton is that she believes all that old crap. Maybe in the old days people thought they were born for the purpose of suffering, but who thinks that nowadays? We're all supposed to enjoy ourselves, aren't we?'

'She says we have no morals. We're not turning out as she expected. She doesn't know what to do with us, we're not developing as we should.'

'I don't see that it's our fault,' Johnny said crossly. 'She made us, didn't she? Goddammit, when is the fucking traffic going to get a move on?'

'That's the point,' Melinda began, then stopped. She felt utterly miserable and confused, and the fumes from the waiting cars were making her sleepy and sick, as if a giant extermination chamber had been set up by a willing population on the pretty wasteland surrounding the city. 'I mean, she says we're behaving as if we didn't believe she *did* make us. As if we had made ourselves. She's afraid for us, Johnny.'

109

'What did she make you think?' Johnny asked suspiciously. He got up and strolled to the bonnet of the car and leaned on it in a romantic attitude, so that for a moment Melinda saw him in a Gothic landscape, the polished metal around him gleaming blue and black as rocks and the haze of the exhaust rising at his feet like vapours from a valley far below. She quoted a few lines:

I deserve, and so does he and so do all the rest of us, a changing in our attitudes to this sick world we live in. If we cannot find God again, then we must learn to love and trust one another. This century has seen enough pain and strife to last out the millennium. Johnny has changed, from the brash youth . . .

'Oh God, not that again!' Johnny lit up a cigarette and gazed furiously at the traffic, as if hoping to detect a current in the still metal, a whirlpool where he might plunge and disappear for good. 'No wonder we've had a hard time of it, Melinda. People used to blame God for all this sort of thing and now we've only each other. She asked too much of us, that's what. Next time I see her she goes, and that's an end to the matter.'

A faint roar in the distance signalled the starting up of a thousand engines, the roll of wheels as the traffic started to move again. Melinda climbed into the car, and Johnny got in beside her and switched on the ignition. In front of them cars laden with boats and camping equipment and food began to edge forward. Johnny laughed and pushed a cassette into the player. The voices of the Supremes flooded from their windows on to the golf course and the rows of low houses beyond.

'Cheer up Melinda, don't lose your nerve! We're not going to settle down in Dorset, whatever she may think!'

The traffic gathered speed and Melinda sat back, glad now that the disturbing thoughts were fading from her mind and Johnny seemed to be in control again. She liked him best when he was like this – indeed it was their only hope of a future, that Mrs Houghton should vanish from their lives and leave them free to make their own decisions. She felt less frightened than before, confident almost that she would become a completely different person once the deed was done. She smiled at him, and laid a hand tentatively on his arm.

110

'Individual acts of violence *can* pay off,' Johnny shouted above the din of the Supremes. 'Especially when there's no alternative, eh Melinda?'

'I get too used to things as they are and I stick to them,' she admitted. 'Johnny, where are we going to if it's not to Dorset?'

'You'll see.'

Soon the characters were in open country. The cars spread out over the great fan of motorways that cover the South-west of England. Johnny and Melinda spoke only once for the rest of the drive – this when they saw a man walking slowly and determinedly along the verge in the direction of London. He was tall and gaunt and stripped to the waist, his grey hair gathered in a pigtail at the nape of his neck and his body tattooed with strange signs. He carried a placard, and as they rushed past Melinda read: THE TIDES HAVE TURNED, BEWARE THE TIDES ... She turned to Johnny and burst out laughing.

'Isn't that strange, Johnny? I kept saying something about the tides in that last scene Mrs H. put us in. She couldn't understand it nor could I. What do you think this means?'

Johnny steered the car at maximum speed into an Exit marked Gate 39. They flew down the narrow road and into a maze of twisting lanes.

'No idea. Some freaks from the Sixties I suppose. I thought they'd starved to death ages ago.'

Melinda sat silent and thoughtful as the car roared between the hedgerows and slowed at last in front of a white house set in a fringe of trees.

Mrs Houghton was beginning to realize she was in the process of marrying Mr Poynter. The pale, suffering features of the late Mr Houghton melted beneath Poynter's square, ordinary face, with its hint of stubbornness about the chin and the military blue eyes that sat perched on either side of his nose like monocles, the deep lines of experience and grief that ran down the sides of his face seeming to hold them there like black cords. Poynter's stern, narrow shoulders replaced those of her loved husband. An un-pleasant nasal twang, reminiscent of Cridge at his most pre-sumptuous, spoke the holy vows. She turned to him in horror, and found herself firmly kissed on the mouth. She screamed soundlessly, but was unable to wake up. Poynter kissed her again, this time to a discreet round of applause from the guests in the chapel, and they walked out into the sunlight and the con-gratulations. They went to the Front Room and cut the cake, and as Cecilia flinched from the furnishings, turning in her faintness from side to side, calling mutely for sympathy at the imposition of the aspidistra and the great draped piano and the antimacassars that bore the marks of heads also turning from side to side in boredom and despair at the institution of marriage, he clasped her hand and promised her the best interior decorator money could buy. She screamed inaudibly at him once more, and the photographer's flash went, recording her gape and Poynter's complacent smile. How could this have come about? She struggled to regain her room, and Johnny and Melinda somewhere by now on the motorway to the West, but the sun continued to flood into the Front Room and children and dogs ran about, and, most nightmarish of all, she thought she recognized the late Mr Houghton's aunt, dressed as she had been for the previous wed-ding and frowning disapproval over a glass of champagne. There was a toast, and speeches. Mrs Houghton gathered she had now become First Lady of this intolerable place, and cursed her early welcome of the dream. She swore, when she woke, that she would go and give the wretched little upstart a piece of her mind. Meanwhile, she found she was being led out on to the lawn again, and awarding a prize in the point to point, and discussing the honeymoon eagerly with her new groom. Apparently they were to go beyond the walls of the City and explore Mr Poynter's invented England. Nothing could have disgusted Cecilia Houghton more. Only a man like Poynter could have the audacity to tamper with the ancient monuments and lop off the tops of trees to suit his own convenience. She bitterly regretted her self-indulgence in the afternoon, and her weakness in abandoning her characters and daydreaming of the happy days that had led to the writing of *On Second Thoughts*. She threw out her arm, in a last attempt to fight off the inevitable ending of the wedding day, and struck Mr Poynter in the face.

When Mr Poynter paid no attention to this assault, Mrs Houghton felt hopeful – that he was perhaps in a dream separate to hers and unaware of her presence there, imagining perhaps his first wedding and blissfully oblivious to the fact that she in no way resembled Mrs Poynter – and defeated, recognizing the strange ability of husbands to ignore complaints on the part of their wives. She raised her fist again (for surely, on the wedding day, this behaviour would provoke some reaction), and then stopped, falling back as Poynter had done, into the bulk of the crowd. A gasp went up, and Mrs Houghton joined in it. For the women had appeared at the french windows, and the guns were going off, and some of the guests lay dead and injured already on the lawn beneath the cedar tree. Mrs Poynter was visible there, her eyes wild and hair streaming. A shocked murmur followed the gasp, and Mrs Houghton realized the first Mrs Poynter had made an appearance amongst the naked hordes. The cry of 'Bigamist' went around. She woke in a sweat, and grasped at the pages by the typewriter. On a day like this, it would hardly be surprising to find that Johnny and Melinda had disappeared from the motorway altogether. She must get back into the scene at once. It was then, when she realized that Block had come down

113

for once and for all, that the characters had slipped off into some unknown Exit and might possibly never be recaptured, that she ran in her rage to the door of Mr Poynter's room. It was his fault, and he would pay for it. Yet when she saw him, in Miss Scranton's room and lying it seemed right on top of her, and the blood flowing from Miss Scranton's eye, Mrs Houghton felt jealousy for the first time in her life. She stood with Mrs Routledge and glared at him. He looked up at her in fear. After a while of standing there in a wifely position, arms folded over the stomach and head held high, Mrs Houghton marched back into her room and put a fresh sheet of paper in the machine. She decided to invent another character, a rival for Melinda, and she began to write. The maddening girl took shape, and as evening fell over the Westringham Hotel and Mrs Routledge went heavily about her cold supper, and Mr Poynter struggled back to his new quarters, his new marriage ruined, and Miss Scranton went smugly to the washbasin to prepare herself for the evening ahead, Mrs Houghton wrote on at increasing speed.

Evening in the Westringham was a time when the fullness of life elsewhere most made itself felt to the inhabitants, and not least to Mrs Routledge herself: it was thin and mean here, so grey and lacking in body it scarcely seemed to need the candle-shaped electric light bulbs which shed a faint aura from the wall brackets in the dining-room; and a daylight as uninspiring appeared always to be lurking in the hall, impatient for dawn and the end of the pretence of night. There could be no festivities here, for the darkness was not thick enough to dispel with merriment. Masks and disguises would easily have been laughed off, there was no cover for surprise. In the perpetual sour twilight objects lacked perspective, and became arbitrarily large or small, like the shadowless things seen while undergoing anaesthesia. The seasons never suggested themselves in this light. Thus, time went slowly and also at a fantastic lick, the artificial passions of the occupants providing the brilliant glare and deep chiaroscuro that were lacking in the place. Mrs Routledge felt, since the arrival of Mr Rathbone's note, that an age had passed and that yet another would have to be endured before she saw him. At the same time, she fussed prematurely over the party, laying out the cocktail biscuits – and a packet of Japanese seaweed that Cridge had bought, she was uncertain if they would do or not but they might conceivably be all the rage – in the glass containers rescued from the basement where he lay. She polished glasses, and tucked the gin under her desk. If only it could be tonight! It was as much as she could do to get on with the supper in hand, lay out the dry ham on plates and a crooked quarter of tomato, a triangle of silver cheese with its accompanying flaking cracker, sardines and cold tinned corn which boasted as hors d'oeuvres. What must Mr Rathbone be doing tonight! As she went from kitchen to dining-room, seeing at every step the proof of Cridge's disgusting habits – a sliminess of the kitchen floor that looked as if an ice tray of saliva had been taken from the fridge and left to melt there, a terrible furriness about the cloth that held the cutlery, a slight heaving and ticking even from the portion of brown carpet beneath the residents' tables, suggesting a form of life too primitive to dare come out and meet the uncertain day. Mrs Routledge dreamed of his engagements and saw herself escorted by him on an evening that was dark and full of mystery and delight. He would be dining with a political hostess, and in her house the candles would be red and fluted and the red wine warmed in fat decanters. After dinner he would sit in her conservatory (Mrs Routledge heard a zither, and changed it to violins) and sip brandy from a glass that stretched his fingers. Then he would rise, leaving the political conversation she found hard to imagine – for in his hands England could come to no harm, and she only hoped he had a firm rein on it – and make his way to a nightclub, where he would dance until bright sunlight succeeded the profound blackness in which he swam with such elegance. Mrs Routledge saw no greyness in Mr Rathbone's life. She knew, when he came, he would bring with him the glamour of the civilized urban evening. She smelt martinis and gardenias and saw the coloured postcard of Manhattan her sister had sent her once. Her life would be transformed by him. She would leave the nursery meals, the faded faces and chewing jaws of the occupants of the Westringham. But first – and she knew this as she passed the dresser in the dining-room, with its Dutch tiles and spotted mirror, and doors that had a way of bulging open as she neared it, as if it were trying to entomb her with the mats and the greasy Christmas decorations – first she must invent a mystery for herself. As she was not enough for him. She stood by the dresser and stared calmly at the face behind the tarnished spots in the glass, which gave her the appearance of a sufferer from bubonic plague. She was stout, and her piled hair could not last an evening out without coming down about her shoulders. Her skin had an oniony look. It was too late now to try the beauty treatments which would no doubt be recommended by Mrs Houghton. Her mystery must be psychological, a compensation for the perspectivelessness of her surroundings. She thought on, and hit on one. It took her to the top of the steps leading down to the basement. She called out.

Cridge was lying on his mattress. He was listening to the radio. An enamel basin containing bread and milk lay at his elbow. The range of cracked opaline pots in which he relieved himself stood on a low table, with one leg missing, at the mattress's end. He heard the call and collapsed his elbow so that he lay flat, both eyes closed under the light from the dim bulb above. A spreading damp stain on the wall by his head suggested a leakage from his brain on to the collapsing plaster. He held his breath, as if he had just died there.

'Cridge!' Mrs Routledge's legs came firmly down the steps. 'Cridge, there's another instruction I need to give you now.'

Cridge sat up suddenly. The radio in his hand whined and hissed.

'It's my day off, Mrs Routledge.'

'I know, I know. It's about the party tomorrow night.'

Mrs Routledge sat down on the end of the mattress by the opaline pots and coughed loudly.

'Can't you empty these things tonight, Cridge? It's perfectly terrible down here, you know.'

'Thursday's their day,' Cridge pointed out. 'Will that be all then?'

'Of course not.' Mrs Routledge remembered that Cridge's co-operation would be needed if her plan were to succeed, and managed an arch smile despite the proximity of the pots. 'I just want to ... well to jog your memory Cridge, if you don't mind.'

Cridge knew what this meant and that there were yet more fabrications of their past together to be spun. But this was not permitted on a Wednesday and his eyes closed stubbornly again.

'It was when you were a stable boy at our place,' Mrs Routledge began. 'At Jonkers ...'

'There's a funny bit of news on the News,' Cridge said in a feeble, ill voice.

'At Jonkers,' Mrs Routledge went on, 'you remember that fateful summer when the head groom went down with pneumonia

117

and Daddy was so absolutely frantic that we wouldn't be able to go over to Longchamps and then down to Monte . . .'

'It said there's some funny mix-up with the tides,' Cridge persisted. 'They been stuck out or something. Now how could that happen, I do wonder?'

'The tides?' Mrs Routledge shrugged. 'Something to do with the fishermen on strike I daresay. Are you listening, Cridge?'

'Yes, Miss Amanda.' Cridge's eyes half opened and he was resigned, propped on his elbow and listening, but with his left hand feeling under the mattress for what he had written that afternoon, a document Mrs Routledge should certainly not see. She stared at him suspiciously as he did this.

'What have you got in there, Cridge? You're not hoarding food, are you?'

'No, no, Miss Amanda. At Jonkers, like you said. Yes, that summer. Go on.'

'We ran off together.' Mrs Routledge spoke slowly and succinctly. 'It was a hot summer and Daddy went ahead to Paris to make the arrangements. We were thrown a lot into each other's company. The paddocks. And the gallops. One night when the haymakers were having their festivities in the field . . .'

'Wait a minute,' Cridge sat bolt upright, inadvertently pulling the tattered exercise book from its hiding place as he did so. 'What's this?'

'We eloped! We couldn't help ourselves. My two brothers followed us and you shot one of them dead. We reached Gretna but by then I had decided you were too much below me in rank and I refused to marry you. You were on the run, of course, wanted for murder, and for the rest of my life I have paid for that early mistake. I have sheltered you here. Mr Routledge was let into the secret, but he lost respect for me when he was told and our marriage was a fiasco. Have you got that?'

Cridge was silent a while. Then he sighed. He slid the exercise book under his body and lay stiffly on it, as if it might bite him.

'Which brother did I shoot?' he asked in a weary tone. 'The one you said used to ride me round the lawn and pretend I was a horse? Andrew, was it?'

'Yes, Andrew. I may tell this to Mr Rathbone and I hope you will remember correctly, Cridge.' Mrs Routledge poked him in the side and Cridge moved uneasily over his subversive literature. 'Now I want to know what is in that book, please. We can't have secrets at the Westringham, you know!'

'It's a story I'm writing,' Cridge replied. His voice was feeble again and he lay hunched, his few muscles ready for the attack that was bound to come. But Mrs Routledge rose. She laughed unpleasantly and strode away from the opaline containers, to the foot of the stairs.

'Trying to imitate Mrs Houghton, are we? Ape our betters? Well Cridge, see to it you remember what I told you tonight.'

'We eloped,' Cridge repeated. His thumb slid over the volume knob of the radio and a voice was distinguishable amidst the hissing. It sounded excited, but not as excited as that of a disc jockey announcing a new record, and the measure of seriousness and agitation in its tone caused both Cridge and Mrs Routledge to assume a listening expression and stay still.

'The tide has suddenly turned,' came the announcement. 'After twenty-six hours of suspense, water is pouring in over the beaches. At some resorts it is reported to have overshot the mark causing flooding and danger to property. A report from . . .'

'What a fuss about nothing!' Mrs Routledge sniffed and began to climb the stairs. 'I'll see you tomorrow then, Cridge.'

The old man nodded. Mrs Routledge's footsteps sounded ponderously above in the dining-room and the bell went for supper. With a trembling hand Cridge pulled out the exercise book and opened it where a pencil lay in wait between two pages. It was his last try. Since the attempt on Mrs Houghton's life had failed in Norfolk, he realized the hopelessness of individual acts of violence, the necessity for theory and a plan of action. Yet Johnny and Melinda seemed incapable of destroying their creator – she could too easily move them from place to place – and Cridge had come to see that it was up to him to remove both Mrs Houghton and Mrs Routledge from the world. He had come to understand Mrs Houghton's power and was determined to use it. It was a long time since he had read or written anything, but he was sure the style counted for little and it was the intention of the author that mattered when it came to dictating the lives of others. He lifted the page to his weak eyes and deciphered what he had ordained so far.

Cridge's Book

'Twas full moon and in the castle the ancient curse of the Houghtons and the Routledges was now at work. The owls hooted in the North West Tower. The fox came from the nodding wheat and the rooks flew from the chimney stack. The barn was blazing, flames went up into the evil night. Cecilia Houghton lay in her great chamber. Ivy grew on the high walls. The windows had been wrenched in the last lightning bolt from their rotting frames and the black air blew in and the sound of small creatures as they ran for cover could be heard below. Thunder rolled about inside the chamber. The man in the red cloak landed on the window sill. Cecilia saw him and gave a piercing scream. He had one eye only and his dagger he held to the empty socket of the other. He approached the fourposter bed, where ivy grew on the decaying wooden posts. He lowered the dagger to her breast. This was white, and exposed in a chemise. He was about to stab. The owl hooted thrice. The fox went for the seventh time around the moat. The door opened and the maid Routledge came in with tea. The grandfather clock in the spearhung hall beneath sounded midnight and the cupboard door in Cecilia's chamber swung open, showing all the seasons of the year in plaster robes, Time with his scythe behind and their heads falling to the ground as he severed them. Maid Routledge fell to her knees and begged for mercy. The red-cloaked man killed her at a stroke, at the same time as garlanded Spring fell to the scythe. Then repeatedly he stabbed Cecilia. When he was done, he threw their corpses from the room, and there was a thud on the dry earth for the moat had dried out in the summer months. The fox went back to its lair. The owl flew in the window of the dagger-heavy hall and flew at the pendulum of the great clock. The curse was done, for the time being, and the red man leapt from the window. There was no sound as he went. Dawn broke, and the world was grateful for the loss of these two monstrous maids.

Cridge tucked his exercise book away when he had finished reading and nodded in satisfaction. He could hear chairs being dragged from tables on the floor above, and a slight murmur of conversation, and wondered when the bodies of Mrs Routledge and Mrs Houghton would be discovered. Little had Mrs Routledge known, when she had sat on his bed and demanded loyal memories of him, that these were her last moments (he had been surprised, to tell the truth, to see her at all, but supposed the power of the word must take longer in finding its full force than he had imagined). By now, surely, they would be fading away if not actually dead, and he would be a free man. He hoped Johnny and Melinda could be found somewhere in the building and told the good news: it would be tragic if they went on going through the motions of characters in the trilogy when their author no longer existed. This altruistic thought gave Cridge a surge of well-being, and he rose from the bed to go on tip-toe to the foot of the stairs. There was silence from above, and he frowned, drawn by what he knew was a fatal curiosity to go up and examine the scene for himself. Every fibre in his much-invented body told him he should climb out of the basement window, exercise book in hand, and disappear into the night before the police were called to make an investigation of the crime. The discovery of his manuscript could lead only to suspicion and arrest. Yet he climbed the stairs, keeping himself in shadow as much as possible, and peered from the top stair but two at the dining-room, and the tables with the chairs set with their backs to the gape of the evil-smelling basement, and the corner of the door into the hall just visible from where he stood. When he saw what he saw a low groan escaped him, but the guests went on eating unperturbed. The pipes in the Westringham often gave off noises like this. Cridge

123

put his hand over his eyes and felt the first trickle of his tears.

Mrs Routledge was there and was in the act of serving Mrs Houghton with the so-called hors d'oeuvres. Mrs Houghton was smiling graciously up at her. Neither woman gave the slightest impression of ill health – Mrs Houghton, in fact, had blazing eyes and a high colour and as she ladled the cold sweetcorn on to her plate appeared to be staring in a distinctly frightening way at Mr Poynter opposite. Mrs Routledge, satisfied no doubt that her cocktail party the next day was now assured of success, was talking low and fast in the way she had when she felt amply in control of the hotel and her guests. Cridge picked up a few words as his eye roamed round the dining-room, settling forlornly on Jeannette Scranton – who seemed dressed to kill tonight, in a sapphire blue evening gown, perhaps she had got the night of the party wrong – and noting with interest that there was no sign of Miss Briggs yet.

'So we had to economize after the war,' Mrs Routledge was saying to Mrs Houghton. 'It was a question of pulling down the North West Tower at Jonkers and moving the kitchens closer in, you know what I mean. In the old days, when poor Cridge had to bicycle along the labyrinth of passages in the basement at Jonkers, the food was *stone* cold by the time it arrived!'

The North West Tower pulled down! Cridge thought of his faulty manuscript and groaned aloud. So he had set the murder in the wrong place! Poynter shifted uncomfortably in his chair and muttered something about it being high time the plumbing was seen to here. Mrs Houghton flashed an angry glance at him and Jeannette nodded agreement from her table.

'You could have opened it to the public,' Cecilia said. 'It seems such a shame, pulling down part of the country's heritage like that!'

A shame indeed! Cridge cracked the knuckles of his fingers together in rage and exasperation. If there was one thing he had picked up from the novelist in the dreary days of his incarceration in her work, it was that real places must be shown, in order to give a solid background to the actions and emotions of the characters. How could Mrs Routledge and Mrs Houghton have died at the hands of the red-cloaked man when the tower had been razed to the ground twenty years before? His ensuing sigh caused Mr Poynter to throw his knife and fork down angrily and twist in his chair. Cridge sank back into the shadows.

'We thought of that! But Daddy was a little short of cash then.' Mrs Routledge still stood over Mrs Houghton. With her left hand she flung the dish out in the direction of Miss Scranton, who quickly scraped some of the contents off on to her plate before it swung back again.

'And what would have been the point?' Mrs Houghton replied. 'The public would have absolutely ruined it, you know.'

'Too many people in the world nowadays,' said Poynter, who was trying to ingratiate himself with Cecilia. (But he could see it was too late, he would never be forgiven for having been found in Miss Scranton's room.)

'All the ancient monuments are in danger of disappearing,' Mrs Houghton said directly at him. 'All those feet! People who have no interest whatsoever in the site. Just gone there for a day out. It should be rationed!'

'I think that's what Daddy felt about opening the tower,' Mrs Routledge put in. 'He saw the future, decided it was better to pull the lovely place down, you know.'

Miss Scranton sipped at her glass of water. Now she felt that Mr Poynter had long been suppressing his true feelings, that he had come out into the open this evening, she saw the night ahead with pleasure and anticipation. She was sure something could be done about the horrible women in the City: once two people find happiness, as she and Mr Poynter were bound to do, such obstacles simply had to melt away.

'Schoolchildren need to visit these important sites,' she said in a low voice. 'I'm sure Mr Poynter agrees with me there. How otherwise can they learn about the country's past glory and feel confidence in the achievements of their own lives?'

'Where's Miss Briggs?' Mrs Routledge said suddenly, for talk of the glorious heritage had brought her to mind. 'It's not like her to be late, is it?'

'In my view,' Mrs Houghton said, 'everyone who wants to climb Snowdon should be made to carry a bag of fifty pounds of earth. Then maybe they'd think twice about it!'

'I quite agree,' Mr Poynter said.

There followed a silence. An idea began to creep into Cridge's head. There was only one solution to the riddle of the failure of his manuscript to have the desired effect on these terrible women. It was not yet published! It lay in his exercise book, embryonic, impotent, while he expected the simple writing down of the words to change his world for him. What would the Gospels have been if they had not been copied and inscribed and printed and taken over the world . . .

'What was that?' Mr Poynter asked testily.

'It sounds as if Cridge is doing something in the basement,' Mrs Routledge said. 'It's Thursday tomorrow of course, and what with the party he has probably decided to . . . well, you know, to empty the pots.'

'I should hope so too.'

'And here's Miss Briggs,' cried Mrs Routledge, who could see that the scene she had witnessed earlier in Miss Scranton's room had caused tensions between the three of them and this must at all costs be avoided before the party. 'Well, Miss Briggs, I thought perhaps you weren't going to join us for dinner tonight?'

Cridge, on the floor below, only listened with a part of himself to the sounds in the dining-room as he thrust the exercise book inside his shirt and prised open the basement window, the frame rotting and the frosted glass panes opening out into the area where the rubbish stood, this channel of filthy concrete having given him the inspiration for the moat and open casements of his fictional tower. He crept through the aperture, a leg went down on to rubbish, damp and compressed as leaf mould.

'But this is impossible! Miss Briggs, I'm sorry . . . Well I simply wasn't expecting this at all . . . No. Do forgive me . . . Of course . . .'

Cridge paused, half way on his urgent quest for a publisher. A male voice that by no stretch of the imagination belonged to Mr Poynter was ringing out on the floor above.

'Please don't put yourself out,' it was saying. 'I'm afraid all this has been a bit of a shock . . . what was that, dear lady? To-morrow night? What was tomorrow night? I wonder if you would be kind enough to tell me where I am?'

A wondering smile spread over Cridge's features. He heard Mrs Routledge make the stumbling introductions.

'Mrs Houghton, Mr Rathbone. Miss Scranton, Mr Rathbone. Mr Poynter, Mr Rathbone. Miss Briggs . . . of course . . . you seem to . . . you know. And you're in the Westringham. As was arranged for tomorrow evening, Mr Rathbone. Miss Briggs, when you bumped into Mr Rathbone and brought him along, I'm afraid you must have been feeling a tiny bit vague.'

The anger and the graciousness mixed brought a gulp of laughter to old Cridge's throat. He swung his other leg over the window sill and crawled through the refuse to the area steps.

'Cridge! Come up here at once! The party is tonight after all! Cridge!'

But by the time Mrs Routledge reached the basement her trusted servant had gone, manuscript in hand. She went back up to the dining-room and the embarrassing scene there and put as good a face on it all as she could.

Marcus Tapp was on his way to London. It hadn't taken long, once the tide had turned and the strange woman who resembled Moira's mother had nodded meaningfully at him on the esplanade at Frinton, for Marcus to run upstairs to his room at the White Horses, shed his waiter's outfit and clip on the grey pigtail needed as a distinguishing mark for his new role as prophet and revolutionary of these stirring times. He stripped to the waist, despite the snowy seaside weather, and painted his torso with initials and astrological signs. He left a brief note for the manager, explaining that the hotel would soon be under water and that this was due to the revisionism and materialism of the White Horse Group; and within ten minutes of the first glimpse of the grey waves rolling in at unaccustomed speed over the beach he was on the main road, his thumb held aloft and the lorries passing him by with no more than a hurled gibe or insult from the drivers at his mute request to be taken into London by them.

Because of this reluctance on the part of the public to hear Marcus's revelations, he soon found that his route was more tortuous than he had hoped. An old lady in an ancient Ford van – thinking he was a Seventh Day Adventist perhaps, or a member of some new sect which would reassure her that the world would end at roughly the same time as she did, took him right across the South of England and deposited him in Devon, where she was planning to spend a week bottling jam with her sister. Although she never went at more than twenty miles an hour, she contrived somehow never to stop; and poor Marcus, for several hours, was put in the unpleasant position of having to decide whether to jump out and risk minor injuries at this historical moment or to go on answering her fatuous questions until she was finally ready to let him go. He decided on the latter, it would be galling to find oneself laid up in a cottage hospital somewhere while all the comrades were reaping the reward of their long years of patience in the metropolis, and stiff from the jolting of the little car and the old lady's incomprehension of his explanation of British history in the twentieth century, he set out anew from a small village on the edge of Dartmoor, resolving this time to walk rather than be blown hither and thither like a dandelion seed by any passing motorist.

Two good omens however cheered Marcus as he made his way to the city. The first was a Belgian truck, with a driver who stopped for the striding, painted figure without having to be asked and nodded vigorously every time Marcus spoke of the Revolution, although this was the only word of English he seemed able to understand. The second – and this was when Marcus was on the grass verge once again, having found to his disgust that the driver was keen to kiss him on the lips at each slowing down of the traffic at a roundabout or intersection, was when he glimpsed two familiar faces speed past him in the direction of the coast. Even if they were going the wrong way Johnny and Melinda were excellent portents at this particular time. He had followed their exploits in Czechoslovakia and Cuba and Bolivia, and had sympathized with them when their author had forced them to become the feeble puppets of her bourgeois individualistic will. The middle volume, in fact, he had thrown in the fire at his aunt's house, where it had lain against the bars of flickering gas and burned slowly, giving off a sickening smell and hastening that woman's decision to leave all she had to the cats; seeing them now, for however brief a time, and with expressions of such resolve on their faces, showed they were not imprisoned indefinitely in some dreary home and marriage of her making; that the right people were at least coming out from their hiding places and demonstrating their determination to fight the system and survive.

Marcus's spirits lifted as he trudged on. He was several times given short lifts and was in no way discouraged by being dumped down abruptly when he let his new discovery be known. A prophet in his own country . . . he spoke of the menacing stillness of the tide, its sudden reversal, and the need to be prepared for the final confrontation. Seabirds seldom glimpsed in the rural depths of Somerset and Dorset bore out his words, flying like albatrosses above the bonnets of the cars and trucks he was allowed for a short time to occupy. At one point, as he was leaving a market town in a Rover driven by a commercial traveller, he even spotted a distant swirl of water, grey against the ploughed fields and short grass of the downs, but his benefactor shook his head, gave an uncomfortable laugh, and shot Marcus on to the verge once more, where he walked on patiently. His only anxiety was that the tide might engulf him before he could reach his comrades and break the news. But by a stroke of luck – and by the time it came to him Marcus was tired and sweating, the painted initials and signs of the zodiac running together in an inky mess on his chest – he was carried right into the west of London by a kind deaf man in a Vauxhall, and let out by the doors of the Kensington Hilton. Backing away from the glaring doorman, he went to the nearest telephone kiosk and reached in his jeans' pocket for his address book. From their hidden nests the old friends and sympathizers would rally to his call. They would storm the communications centres, in all probability, and inform the masses of the great turning of the tide. Marcus would be their spokesman – even, though such a term would not be used, their leader. He smiled to himself as he dialled, still watched with suspicion by the doorman of the Hilton, for it was a cold, sunless day and the nakedness of his torso brought glances of surprise even from his potential followers as they strolled aimlessly past the box where he stood.

Marcus's calls were met not with astonishment but, he noted, incredulously, with a lassitude that ill became the firebrands of former years. Some of them asked him over for a meal or a cup of coffee, and when he got there laughed at his smudged chest and offered shirts and sweaters and the money for a ticket home. He informed them of the tides, and the impending Revolution, and some replied that everything rested with the Trade Unions now, others that they belonged to a group whose initials would always be denied him, others still that they were concentrating on the production of pornographic theatre in the West End for the furtherance of their own fortunes and the fortunes of the real

Revolution when it came. None believed his descriptions of the hunch that had come to him so strongly at the esplanade in Frinton-on-Sea: they told him not to trust in instinct in these matters, to return there and continue his studies of Marx and Engels until the time was ripe; one young revolutionary, middle-aged now and with a heavy stomach under his caftan, offered him a job in an antique market off the Portobello Road. After several hours, dispirited and exhausted, Marcus found himself out on the street again and wandering the crumbling area around the motorway to the West. He called on a squat and was for a moment cheered by what he saw, but they seemed as uninterested there in his tale of the tides as his other friends had been. He was offered accommodation, and went off with a heavy heart in the direction of Notting Hill. It was then he remembered that Moira lived in the neighbourhood – at least, she had in the days of his love for her, and he turned into the familiar crescent, went with his last strength to the door, the many bells, some of them pulled out and hanging on their wires above the rotting plaster, and searched blindly for her name. He found it, and pressed hard on the half-disconnected bell. As he waited, he scanned the street, and saw with his tired eyes an old man climb the area steps of the next-door house and dart off down the road as if the devils were after him. It was dark, and the lighting in the street was bad, and Marcus did no more than rub his eyes and shrug his shoulders. Moira let him in and stood with a grave expression on the threshold. She said it was the group meeting at her place tonight and if he wanted to see her he should have let her know. Marcus tried to tell his story – and by now it was beginning to seem unlikely – and Moira laughed once before looking serious again. She said the tides were indeed turning, and he would be the first to know it. After this cryptic announcement she went in and slammed the door in his face. For some minutes Marcus stood on the doorstep in complete dejection. In the weak white light from the street lamps his torso had taken on a zebra-esque air, white and black stripes encompassing his body above his jeans. His eyes smarted from the day's travels and his legs ached. He thought of the squat address he had been given, but felt too tired to find his way through the maze of streets to the other side of Notting Hill. He looked up and down the road and listlessly examined the faded sign hanging outside the next-door house, the house from which the old man had recently bolted into the night. He picked out the word UNCHES ND TEAS BED ND BREAK, and stumbled on to the pavement and up the step to the door. It was a swing door and he pushed it. He found himself in a dingy hall. Loud voices came from a dimly glimpsed dining-room beyond. It was thus that Marcus Tapp, one of those unfortunate instances of a perfect stranger picking up the dream of another miles away and finding the course of his life changed, his steps drawn inexorably to the dreamer, his account of his dream never believed because it lacks the authenticity of the original vision, landed up in the Westringham Hotel. And in the midst of an impromptu party given for Mr Rathbone by Mrs Routledge, proprietress of the establishment and none too pleased to welcome Tapp in at that inauspicious hour.

Mr Rathbone, like the unfortunate Marcus, was the victim of a stranger's dream, but he was responsible for the Westringham – and, it could be said, for the dreams of the inmates by upholding a society which produces those dreams; nevertheless he deserved some sympathy on that Wednesday night. Mrs Routledge, whose fantasy he had been for so long, came as an unpleasant surprise to him. Miss Briggs seemed to have a power over him – she had brought him here, after all, without his expressing the least desire to accompany her – and his knighthood, the apex of his career, had been performed by her, an impersonator of Her Majesty. She was smiling at him proudly as he nibbled nuts and sipped at the warm gin and tonic provided. He felt, for the first time in his life, baffled and confused by the events of the day, and although an outsider would have awarded a prize to Mr Rathbone for the calm and composure with which he discussed cricket with Mr Poynter, acquaintances in common with Mrs Houghton, and the urgent need to reform the comprehensive school system with Miss Scranton, he was in fact desperate to return to his tiny flat and his large wife, to ask her why she had disappeared so mysteriously at the gates of the Palace, and to gain reassurance in himself by going for a stroll with her in the park and seeing how incomparably bigger he was than the rest of the population. Here, in the dining-room of the Westringham, the other members of the party were in some peculiar way neither smaller nor greater than himself. It was as if they existed on a different plane, and there was nothing he could measure himself against. The power of their dreams, perhaps, had removed them from his world – and as a consequence he felt uncomfortable and unreal. As he absentmindedly replied to Mrs Routledge – she was clinging to his arm and winking up at him over the rim of her glass – he tried to reconstruct the unusual happenings of the afternoon. Lines of concentration appeared on his wide brow. Mrs Routledge tittered and dug her nails into his sleeve.

'I'm not surprised you're a mite shocked, Mr Rathbone. But you know how it is. Young, romantic love. Daddy perhaps a little too taken up by his horses. A June night with the haymakers in the field celebrating beneath the full moon. The whole heart of the universe seeming to beat there under the dark sky . . .'

'Yes, yes, dear lady.' Mr Rathbone thought back and his brow turned to a network of wrinkles. He had arrived at the Palace in his Rolls, smiling to himself at the practical joke played on him in the park by some young prankster who had been to the funfair and printed up an abdication story for a few pence in a booth. He wouldn't have been taken in, of course, if he hadn't been pre-occupied, slightly nervous even: a knighthood was a big event. There was the usual small crowd of small people outside the Palace and he had driven in unnoticed, in that wonderful way that was so English – not a cheer even, or a curious face. He had dismounted at the back entrance and gone up a flight of red carpeted stairs. There were flunkeys about and he had been ushered into an ante-chamber. It was indicated to him that he should wait.

'Probably it was because Daddy would have disapproved so terribly of Cridge. He had a peerage in mind for me, you know how fathers are, Mr Rathbone. Anyway, we decided then and there to elope to Gretna Green. I didn't take a stitch with me!'

After what seemed a very long time the wide doors at the far end of the ante-chamber were thrown open. Mr Rathbone, his legs weaker than he would have cared to admit, walked into the Throne Room. A small figure was on the throne under the canopy of red and gold. He bowed three times. It was when he came up for the third time that he saw the twisted, cruel faces of the Van Dyck portraits, the dead and rotting animals by the quiet lakes in the great pastoral scenes, the evil mushroom cloud that hung over and partially obscured Poussin's beautiful Arcadia. He coughed loudly.

'Such a close night,' cried Mrs Routledge, who imagined her guest had smelt Cridge's pots – (and then and there, in the midst

134

of her invented romance with him, swore she would throw him on the street when he returned). 'We have problems with the drains in this street, Mr Rathbone. Is there anything you can do to help us?'

'As soon as I finish the trilogy,' Mrs Houghton was saying to Mr Poynter, 'I shall of course be going off to recuperate with relatives in Worcestershire.'

'Of course, of course.' (Mr Poynter was miserable; he prayed only that the dream would right itself tonight. But this seemed unlikely, with Miss Scranton standing by him, her eyes burning and the gin bottle tipping into her glass each time he looked.)

Mr Rathbone left Mrs Routledge in mid-sentence and went over to Miss Briggs. When he had seen her on the throne, he had done nothing – he had knelt even! – she had knighted him and he had let her! He found this hard to believe, but it was true. And while he was kneeling there, his mind spinning, every fibre of his being telling him he must be suffering from an hallucination, he would look up again in a minute and see the features of his dear monarch – there had been a rushing sound, a blurring of the vision, and he was in a dingy room with this woman, she tucking a rusty sword back into its scabbard and a bell ringing downstairs which she told him meant they were summoned to go down. And he had obeyed her! He went now and stood over her, but in her disquieting way Miss Briggs, although a small woman by any standards, seemed in no way dwarfed by him. For a moment Mr Rathbone wondered if she could indeed be the Queen, to whom his normal criteria of size obviously did not apply.

'Miss Scranton, I have sad news for you,' Mrs Routledge said, skirting the bulging dresser and going to her without further ado. 'There has been trouble at the Westringham lately, as you are clearly aware, and one of the matters I have decided to bring up with Mr Rathbone is the necessity for your departure, the question of our legal situation here if you decline.'

'May I ask what you are doing impersonating Her Majesty?' Mr Rathbone said to Miss Briggs. His heart beat too loudly for his own comfort as he asked her this, and he looked at her almost imploringly, demanding to be restored to his real world and his wife without delay.

'I have no intention of leaving,' Miss Scranton said loudly and drunkenly. 'You can't get me out of here, you silly old bitch!'

'Miss Scranton, please!' Mrs Routledge shrank. Not only was Cridge missing – no one to hand the nuts and drinks, the pots unemptied, but now there was to be bad language too. What must Mr Rathbone think?

'Let's take a vote on it,' said Mr Poynter suddenly. The drink had also gone to his head – and he had nothing to lose. It seemed pretty clear that a democratically elected majority would eject Miss Scranton, and life would be tolerable again.

'I vote she goes,' said Mrs Houghton, who had materialized by Mr Poynter's elbow, and this gave him a wonderful feeling of confidence. 'Miss Briggs, your vote please?'

'My vote?' Miss Briggs turned her head slowly. 'I am of course not able to vote, Mrs Houghton. I should have thought you'd know that by now!'

'A vote?' cried Mr Rathbone. The nightmare was building up for him. Miss Briggs refused to answer any of his questions. Mrs Routledge was coming towards him with the story of her early love. Mr Poynter was going to ask him technical details about his Rolls again. He reached for the whisky bottle and took a long swig from the neck.

'A lovely informal atmosphere,' cried Mrs Routledge. 'A bottle party! What fun!'

It was at that moment that Marcus Tapp lurched through the swing doors of the Westringham and stood before the assembled guests. In the dim light from the hall his striped, smudged chest gave him the air of a miner up from the pit. His grey pigtail hung over his face. Mrs Routledge gave a short scream.

'One of the workers,' said Mr Poynter, in the voice he used in his City. 'Send him for correction, Struthers.'

'My dear man, what do you want?' Mrs Houghton bustled forward. 'You don't seem terribly well, I must say. Mrs Routledge, is there a drop of soup in the kitchen for this man?'

Tapp advanced into the dining-room. He was drawn like a magnet to Miss Scranton and he stood for a moment before her. Then his head dropped and the pigtail swung before his eyes. When he looked up again, he saw Mr Rathbone. The strength of his hatred was like desire. The two men faced each other and stood in silence.

'Where's the gin?' Miss Scranton said thickly. 'This party is a scandal I don't mind telling you that Mrs Routledge. You want that man, don't you?' She waved wildly in the direction of Mr Rathbone. 'Well if you do dear you'll have to play your cards right. Empty that shit out of the basement for one thing. And supply enough booze for God's sake. It's a scandal, that's all it is.'

The silence grew more dense. Marcus and Rathbone continued to stare at each other in fascinated loathing. Mrs Routledge gave an uneasy little laugh.

'Do try some of this Japanese seaweed, Mr Rathbone. And forgive the intrusion. I'm sure our visitor here has mistaken the Westringham for somewhere else. Can I redirect you at all, sir?'

'I want a room for the night,' Marcus said. 'I'm tired.'

As he spoke, Tapp's legs seemed to give way under him. He fell half on to Mrs Houghton, and was caught by Mr Rathbone before he reached the floor. With the exception of Mr Poynter, who was shocked by the kindness shown to the stranger, and Miss Scranton, who had felt her hackles rise as soon as she saw him, sympathy for Tapp was expressed once it was firmly established that he was one of the world's victims. He was laid out on two chairs in the dining-room while preparations were made for him in Room 26. Marcus Tapp was the first to sleep, and to dream, in the Westringham Hotel that night.

Johnny and Melinda were sitting in the kitchen of their hideaway, the white farmhouse in a fringe of trees hidden in a maze of narrow lanes off Exit 39. For the past hour they had been congratulating themselves on the easiness of their escape, and the possible methods of despatching Mrs Houghton into the next world when they felt like showing their faces again; now, as they sipped tea and looked out at the leafless trees, the bleak spring landscape of grassy banks that looked as if they had been crushed by winter and might not find their form again, they both began to feel aware of a blankness, an emptiness in their lives which, in the days of resisting Mrs Houghton, they had never known. They saw that the interior of the farmhouse was blank and white too: each room had the same proportions, no pictures hung on the walls, and there were no books anywhere. They had welcomed the rooms at first, but now they found the square whiteness oppressive, as if sheets of unused paper were constructed about them; and without admitting it to each other both characters caught themselves hoping for a written word to appear at the cornice, for others to follow it, and for a whole page of their lives to unfurl right across the room and down to the skirting board. The silence, too, was unnerving – and when a tractor started up in a distant field Melinda and Johnny exchanged a quick, surreptitious glance, mistaking the sound for a moment for the familiar rattle of keys. They were free – they were no longer pursued – but the impetus to murder their creator seemed to have gone with the achievement of their freedom. Melinda felt an increasing sense of guilt, the need to apologize to Mrs Houghton for deserting her like this and a plea to be taken back. Johnny, still maintaining an air of bravado, chain-smoked and drummed with his fingers on the table, traits which had been written into him at an early stage and which he knew it would take a long time to throw off.

'She must have thought of something,' Melinda said at last. 'What will she do without us, Johnny? I mean, will her career be finished, d'you think?'

'People will go on believing in her for a time,' Johnny said. 'There's still more incense laid at her altar than any other. But they'll forget . . . she doesn't belong to this age, you know. What's the matter Melinda, are you feeling guilty again?'

'She didn't really treat us so badly,' Melinda muttered. 'She believed in *us*, after all, and who else will now?'

'No one should believe in us. We don't have any significance. We'll have to change if we're to have any meaning in the modern world.'

Melinda shivered. She got up and crossed the square white kitchen and lowered the blind over the window so that only the bright fluorescent lighting was in the room. The blind was black, like a ruled line of ink against the walls, and she turned from it shuddering again and went back to her chair by the table.

'I don't want to look out at a place I don't belong in. How can we change ourselves, Johnny? Cecilia thought of us as individuals, at least. Surely . . .'

Before Melinda had time to finish, footsteps sounded on the gravel path outside and a key scraped in the door. She jumped to her feet, and Johnny pulled her down again roughly.

'What did I tell you? Give me a guess and I'd say this is our Mrs Houghton's last attempt in the present form to bring us to heel. Keep laughing. It's the only hope.'

Melinda nodded, her eyes wide with terror as the steps pattered across the square hall of the farmhouse and came to the kitchen door. Part of an aria was hummed, and then broken off. The door opened. Melinda clamped her hand across her mouth, forcing out a cross between a laugh and a sob of fear, and Johnny, unable to follow his own advice, rose to his feet and stood dumbfounded. Then he gave a long whistle.

'Well I'm damned! What the hell does she think she's doing this time?'

The girl who stood in the doorway of the overbright kitchen

was at first glance young and attractive, with long black hair, a slender figure, and pretty legs going down into scarlet, pointed shoes. She was wearing a black cardigan and skirt, and a row of pearls hung over her breasts. She stretched out a hand in greeting and Melinda shrank back. Johnny shut his eyes and groaned.

'I am your rival,' the girl said in a low clear voice to Melinda. 'Please fill me in on what is going on here, as I fear I am rather a late arrival on the scene!' Her voice was foreign, French perhaps, and pleasant to listen to. Melinda swallowed hard, and forced herself to walk up to the girl, while Johnny still stood blind, and swaying on his feet.

'Your face . . .' Melinda began. 'I'm sorry . . . but you . . . why do you have no face?'

A smile made itself felt from the blank expanse of skin, oval-shaped, which occupied the space between hairline and neck.

'I think I was being described and the description was broken off in the middle,' the girl said – and for a moment Melinda thought she could see a mouth there, so strong was the desire to see it. 'But I was given words to say . . . and I was set down at this farmhouse so here I am,' she continued. 'If I am to be your rival – your name is Melinda, no? – then I would like to know if I am supposed to take this man from you?' She pointed to Johnny, who opened his eyes and closed them again. 'Is he in love with me? It seems he is not.'

'And what's your name?' Melinda said quickly. She felt Mrs Houghton's power already, a stirring of interest in Johnny for the faceless girl, a sense of tension which made her want to escape from the farmhouse and hide from both of them in the surrounding fields.

'My name is Joa,' the girl said. 'I think I was meant to be Joanna, but she got so angry. She scrumpled me up, you know, and then straightened me out again. Has this ever happened to you?'

'Hasn't it just,' Johnny growled. His eyes were open now and he was appraising the girl, glancing guiltily at Melinda when he had finished. 'Look, Joa, we're all in the same boat now. Melinda and I are on the run from that woman, do you understand? And so are you. So . . .'

'So we all hide out here together,' said Melinda bitterly. 'We might as well sleep in the same bed, eh Johnny?'

'Please!' If Joa had had eyes they would have gone wide in innocence. 'I do not wish to take your husband, Madam. I can assure you of that. I was sent here, you know.'

'He's not my husband,' Melinda snapped. 'That's what we're running away from.'

Joa gave another of her invisible smiles. 'Then if you do not want each other I can surely have a good time with Johnny. I am sorry, I am wrong somewhere?'

Johnny suddenly laughed loudly. 'I know where you come from, Joa. You've been in one of Cecilia's early novels about the au pair running off with the husband, and the anguish of the wife, haven't you? And poor dear Cecilia half remembered you and decided to put you in as a punishment for us. Well Melinda, what did I tell you about that woman's resources when she finds herself with her back against the wall?'

Both Melinda and Johnny read a pout into the girl's face as she answered this.

'It is possible I was in such a situation once. But it was not pleasant for me either and I do not think there was much sympathy shown to me. Will this be the same now? I cannot endure Madam in a rage and I prefer to leave the post.'

'No no.' Melinda went up to Joa and took her by the hand. 'If we're all friends she'll be thwarted. Can't you see that? It's our only hope. Isn't that so Johnny?'

'Indeed it is.' Johnny was looking at Joa greedily by now and despite himself winked and made a movement of the head unmistakably suggesting a visit to one of the square white rooms upstairs. 'Very sensible Melinda and very true,' he went on in a throaty voice.

'We'll all go upstairs together,' Melinda said. She was firm, but her legs trembled beneath her: if she should show jealousy at this point all would be lost and Mrs Houghton would have her way with them for ever. 'I'll lead the way,' she said to Joa. 'The front room don't you think Johnny, with the big bed. It's made up. I noticed that when we arrived.'

'Whatever you say.' Johnny sounded surprised, and was trying to conceal this. 'After you,' he said heartily to Joa. 'Rather fun, don't you think? And I'm sure it's not what's intended!'

Melinda opened the kitchen door, and Johnny and Joa followed her into the hall. They began to climb the stairs. But when they reached the landing, all three stopped in confusion and Johnny let out a shout of rage.

'The bitch! She's trying something else on us now that this hasn't worked!'

Melinda, on looking into the bedroom, found herself laughing at last, and turned to Joa with the laughter still on her lips. But Joa had gone. Only Johnny stood on the landing, and before them, where the bare white-walled bedroom had been, was a tent, multi-coloured and splendid, and two mattresses, side by side on the floor. From the flap in the tent a desert scene showed: white dunes, a line of camels, the topmost branches of a date palm.

'So she's trying all the perfumes of Arabia,' said Johnny quietly. He took hold of Melinda's arm and they went into the tent and sat down.

Mrs Houghton's Fable

There was a young merchant who married the most beautiful girl in the district and immediately after set out with his servants along the road, leaving his guests to feast and dance and his wife to pine in his absence. His companion, Rashid, was concerned about this, and said:

'Why do you leave your wife and friends and go out on the road alone?'

'I have not enough to give her,' the merchant replied. 'My father was a rich man but I am not, and I go to seek my fortune so that she will be the finest wife any man can have.'

A serpent who was lying under a stone by the side of the road heard this and came out from under the stone and spoke.

'You may take my skin for your wife,' it said. 'It is the most beautiful skin of any serpent in the world and she may adorn herself with it. But now you must go back to the wedding feast before more time is lost.'

The merchant took the skin and thanked the snake. 'I will go a little further,' he said to his companion, Rashid. 'I cannot return to my wife with only one offering.'

They went on and as they went a fox who was lying in his earth by the side of the road heard them speak.

'You may take my skin,' the fox said, appearing before them. 'I am old and I have lived long enough and your beautiful wife may adorn herself with it. But you must go back to the wedding feast before more time is lost.'

The fox lay down and died and the merchant cut the skin from its back.

'We will go on a little further,' he said to Rashid. 'For I can see eyes as beautiful as my wife's by the side of the road and she shall have them to wear around her neck.'

143

A peacock, who had heard the merchant speak to Rashid in this fashion, came out into the road and stood before them.

'I have the most beautiful tail in the world,' it said, 'and the eyes are even more beautiful than your wife's. But I shall keep it for myself as you already have enough to offer her. Go back to the wedding feast before more time is lost.'

The merchant killed the peacock and went on down the road with the tail held out before him so that he could not see the road. A group of bandits, thinking the eyes belonged to a marching army, set on the merchant and Rashid and their servants and took them off into the hills. They spent many years in captivity, and when they were released they made their way back along the road where they had met the serpent and the fox and the peacock. The merchant had no offerings for his wife, and he went with a bowed head into the tent he had not seen since the day of his wedding feast.

An old woman came out to greet him.

'What do you want here?' she said. 'I am a widow and the poorest woman in the district. I will wash your feet for you and give you water but more I cannot do.'

While the old woman was washing the merchant's feet she recognized a mark on the sole of her husband's left foot. The merchant and Rashid at the same time recognized the tent and saw that the old woman was the merchant's wife.

'I have nothing to offer you,' said the merchant, who was deeply ashamed.

'And nor have I anything to give you,' the old woman replied.

A serpent and a fox and a peacock came into the tent when they heard the merchant and his wife speak.

'We can give you our skins,' said the fox and the serpent, 'but we cannot give you Time back.'

'You can take the eyes from my tail,' said the peacock, 'but they will not look well on your wife now, for her own eyes have dimmed. If you had hearkened to us on the road you would have had plenty to give to each other. Now, as it is, you will soon die of poverty and old age.'

This came to pass, and, the merchant's wife dying first, the merchant took her eyes as a gift to the peacock. The peacock refused them, saying:

'I will not take human eyes as a gift. They are faded. My eyes see Truth, and that is why they never fade.'

As the fable ended, the tent where Johnny and Melinda had been sitting began slowly to dissolve and the square white walls of the farmhouse bedroom showed through the rich hangings. The smell of camel dung, which had grown ever stronger as the fable was recited through the flap in the tent, became less acute. Melinda sighed in relief.

'She's not going to get us that way,' she said. She spoke with resolve, but her voice was shaken. 'What's she saying? That I'll lose my looks and you'll be an old man if we don't get back on the road and go to Dorset?'

'God knows. I suppose so.' Johnny frowned at the window, where the topmost branches of a date palm were still clearly visible. He looked pale. 'What the hell is she doing to us, Melinda?'

The characters held hands briefly, and as they did so the scene changed again, this time to a first-floor room in what appeared to be a French coastal resort, with the palm clearly outlined beyond a small balcony, and crowds on the beach below. Coloured balls bobbed in the air, and a group of children lay on rubber mattresses in the sea.

I will tear the limbs from your body. I will dive in the gold of your shield. I will pierce your heart and I will gnaw at your entrails. The sea is blue as a kite. The irises of your eyes are iris. I will eat your hair and I will take your vitals in my hands. The balloon of the child is orange like an orange. I will scoop your pupils into the sun. I will dive in the sea which is flat and blue as a balloon.

'Must be translated from the French,' Johnny said gloomily when the voice had stopped and the seaside scene had faded. He got up from the bed and went over to the window, which was returning to farmhouse proportions, the balcony outside disappearing into thin air as he looked out. 'The palm's going, thank God,' he remarked over his shoulder. 'Just some rhododendrons there, and the usual English fields. Well Melinda,

145

what are we going to do? I'm feeling pretty exhausted by now.'
He went back to the bed and lay down and closed his eyes. 'There
isn't much more I can take. How about you? You think we might
as well get back on the road, don't you? Just obey her, admit
defeat?'

'I know what she's doing,' Melinda said. Her voice sounded
sleepy too, and she rolled over and kissed Johnny on the cheek.

'Oh not that!' Johnny half sat in indignation and then slumped
back again. 'Her last resort – perhaps that's what the last scene
was trying to tell us.' He giggled, and ran his fingers through
Melinda's hair. 'Here goes,' he muttered. 'We have to hand it to
her I suppose.'

If they had made love before, it had never been like this. There was
in the passion between the man and woman in the empty house a fire
and a calm that was like a waterfall of stars; the music that sounded in
their ears was that of a great marching crowd, going to demand its
rights from the oppressor; worlds rolled out in front of them, wide
continents and seas with long waves breaking before even there was
land in sight. The sky hung above and round them, the moon faded in
the strong wash of blue. Only their bodies, linked like a god and
goddess of the ether, floated across time and space and belief and
falsehood and burned in the Eternal Fire from whence they came.

'Well well,' Johnny said when this was over. 'She's doing her
best, I'll say that.'

'It was wonderful,' Melinda agreed. 'Better than when she has
the Lawrence influence. Don't you think?'

'Oh I can't stand that,' Johnny agreed. He rose briskly from
the bed, refreshed from the experience, and held out a hand
to Melinda to pull her up.

'I think we better go back to London and find our Cecilia,' he
said. 'Looks to me as if there must be some arrangement we can
come to with her. I mean, if we don't kill her after all, but settle
her in some way . . .'

'But what about that mad old man?' Melinda said. 'He's
determined to do her in, he's probably creeping into her bedroom
now. She won't believe it, of course.'

'No, she thinks he's a stock comic butler,' Johnny agreed. 'It
just wouldn't be done for a lady like herself to be knocked off

by old Cridge. But we should hurry because he might well bring it off this time. And if she died, then where would we be?'

'Where? I thought we were going to be free,' Melinda cried. 'That was the whole point Johnny, surely.'

'Yes. But I have doubts.' Johnny gave a shamefaced smile. 'Suppose we weren't free after all. We'd be stuck forever just before the end of the book. In the traffic jam on the motorway . . . for eternity. Think of that.'

'Yes.' Melinda considered. 'And if we were free it might not be the kind of life we wanted. If we made her change the end . . .'

'So we didn't have to marry,' Johnny said, excited now. 'If it was all left with a question mark, you know. Like the other two volumes.'

'And we could choose whether we were going to be politically involved, or obsessed by each other . . . or even keen gardeners perhaps . . .'

'Exactly. Let's go. And let's hope there isn't the traffic there was coming down,' Johnny added grimly as Melinda took his hand and they ran down the stairs. 'That's my idea of hell.'

'We haven't annoyed Cecilia enough to deserve that for eternity,' Melinda said in a pious tone. The characters climbed into the Ford Anglia, and by carefully choosing small traffic-free roads, made London and the Westringham Hotel in record time.

Climax

That night, as the residents and their victims in the Westringham dreamed – and sleep came to them in a strange fashion, as we shall see – fragments of their dreams escaped into the outside world, where they were ignored or spoken of with contempt and laughter or seen, by the superstitious, and there was an increasing number of these, as portents, omens of evil times to come. The tides, disturbed by the Amazons, did not rise up and engulf the island. But the scientists and the observant members of the population sought in vain for an explanation for the highest flood tide in recorded history, and for the appearance of a moon that was running, so to speak, several days behind schedule; again, because of their inability to explain this, the ranks of the superstitious grew and a great uneasiness made itself felt, though in what ways, apart from the hoarding of food and in coastal towns the boarding up of ground-floor windows, it would be difficult to define. People went about with distracted expressions and with their heads poked forward, looking up suddenly from time to time as if they expected to see something unpleasant but inevitable in the sky. As if to mirror the breaking apart of Mr Poynter's City, friends turned against each other, relationships broke, parents eyed their children with suspicion. The rate of burglary dropped, for it was within their own homes that people stole, and smashed crockery, and expressed their hatred for the world. And, reflecting Mr Poynter's terrible decree that the future tense should be banned, there was a sense of an absolute knowledge of a limited and predictable future while the past, given the status the future had once had, became infinitely rich, and imagined in a thousand ways, and mysterious. Personal pasts were rewritten, and new crimes discovered, and their perpetrators punished for them. The history of the world was seen at sharply contrasting angles and old battles were relived. Almost anything was taken as a portent, but as the future was so definitely known the portents showed only a variety of past evils. It seemed there was no hope left anywhere: future engagements were planned and then abandoned in the pursuit of a re-interpretation of the past. And the dream of the past was being smashed to pieces on all sides and splintered into nightmare.

If the rate of ordinary crime dropped, admissions to mental homes, already overcrowded with the sad and drugged witnesses of the power of conflicting dreams, went up a hundred-fold in these days. On the Wednesday night, when Mr Poynter closed his eyes and Miss Scranton fell asleep on her feet like a statue and Miss Briggs drifted through the gateway of the City in search of her monarch – and Tapp and Mr Rathbone and Mrs Routledge and Cridge and Johnny and Melinda were pulled in after them to their inescapable doom – ambulance men went on strike and asylums closed their doors in the face of the mass of the hallucinated and the distressed and the mad. Faces were seen dangling from streetlamps – women's faces, with matted hair and bloated cheeks. Across the night sky, dancing like wisps across the great blackboard, hieroglyphs of pale cloud spelt out a fateful message to the initiated. Traffic lights gave secret signs, and in the carless streets crowds collected to decipher their meaning. Stone men marched the pavements. A silent mob stood round Buckingham Palace which, it was rumoured, had been abandoned by the Queen and left to rot and cobweb. Remembering their past beliefs, small armies grew and faced each other in paralysed animosity at every crossroads. The whine of the police sirens drew mass confessions from the crowd, and people threw themselves on their knees and begged to be put out of their misery, to be taken to a quiet place and incarcerated there. Not that there was any noise in the streets of London that night: only the agonized, inner screaming of brains invaded by other brains, of falling and fading dreams and the sense of chaos that comes after. Some thought the tides had come up, and saw sheets of water where there was none on the black asphalt. Others saw the monarch on the empty, dark balcony of the palace – like a falling meteor, glittering and then gone. Money turned damp and worthless in wallets and pockets and people threw it on the ground so it lay like sweet wrappers. There was a feeling of expectancy – and the knowledge that there was nothing to expect.

Just before midnight, as more and more people packed the streets and the crowds stood in dense silence – like black banked clouds come down from the sky to press on pavements and gutters and buildings, to create a pressure that could only be resolved by storm, a great rumbling made itself heard somewhere in the distance. At first it was taken for the sound of tanks, and a low groan escaped from the crowd. A million imaginations saw the slowly moving wheels of armoured trucks; a picture, composed by numberless artists, of the forthcoming massacre hung for a second like a giant film screen above the heads of the crowd. The sound grew louder, but no trucks appeared, and in a sibilant whisper the information was conveyed that even on the outskirts of the city there were no trucks to be seen. Then some great demolition scheme was envisaged, and as the rumbling increased in volume the people saw yellow cranes, and the ball that swings into the sides of houses and the fragile, vulnerable walls with rosy wallpaper and cracked washbasins that stand exposed before the next onslaught from the machine. They saw their own houses fall, and heard the sharp meeting of the cannon ball and the outer wall, the trickle, like shifting sand, of dropping plaster as the inner walls subsided. Heads turned, and the horizon was scanned for the cloud of dust that rises into the air and hangs there in place of houses when a street is razed to the ground. But there was none; and soon the whisper went round again that the bulldozers and cranes were lying idle in their yards. Panic swept the crowd, and by the time the sound was recognized as thunder an undertow was dragging it to west London, where the streets were already packed with people. The clouds seemed thicker there, and the noise deafening over the crumbling crescents and curved motorways. The clouds piled up and crashed over the Westringham Hotel and the surrounding streets. When they parted, before gathering force to run together again, a flat black sky could be seen and a thin moon, and cloud women with knotted, wispy limbs dancing on the starless expanse. Eyes, and tresses of hair, and sinewy cloud arms rose and fell above the blanket of thunder cloud. The crowd sighed and pushed further into the streets and stood staring up at the threatening sky. The panic had ebbed away, there was only a sense of watching and waiting. The battle of the clouds began to die down a little, and the first drops of rain fell on the crowd. A window on the first floor of the Westringham opened and a man looked out. Without knowing why, the crowd gave a great shout. The man's head went in and the window closed. The crowd surged round the Westringham, and then stopped. Again, there was a sense of waiting. The rain began to fall more heavily on the crowd.

The cocktail party at the Westringham had not ended; it had changed, to Mrs Routledge's pleasure and bewilderment, to an infinitely superior party somewhere else. Just as Johnny and Melinda and old Cridge, who had fought their way through the crowds to the entrance of the hotel (Cridge muttering with disappointment and clutching his exercise book: on a night like this there was not a publisher to be found in London), appeared at the door, the walls of the dining-room widened and grew taller and panels of a plum-coloured brocade fringed with gold braid stretched out over them, obscuring the soup stains incurred by Mrs Routledge throwing a cup of Heinz tomato at Mr Routledge when he had been too reasonable with her, and the grim shadows of grease and damp, that danced from cornice to dado on the walls nearest the kitchen. The plastic ferns on the residents' tables grew to the noble proportions of potted palms. A chandelier, descending like a small galaxy from the ceiling, threw a flattering light on Mrs Routledge's face and bosom, which she saw now was encased in a blue satin off-the-shoulder gown; and the guests, also improved in appearance by the lighting and the rich surroundings, seemed all of a sudden more relaxed and animated, as if the change of ambience had given them a new lease of life and they were prepared to stay at the party all night. Mr Rathbone, who had broken away from a long conversation about the economic crises facing the country with Mr Poynter, was in the midst of presenting a piece of paper to his hostess when the decor changed its tone. He stopped, puzzled and irritated by the disturbance, but decided to finish his sentence nonetheless. After his unpleasant experiences in the Palace that afternoon, he had determined to pay less attention to outward appearances, and simply get on with the matter in hand. These tricks were clearly sabotage, and probably the work of Marcus Tapp, who was at present mercifully unconscious on two chairs in the corner: when the business with Mrs Routledge was done, Mr Rathbone had every intention of calling the police and getting him sent to prison for treason and a host of other crimes as well.

'So as you see Mrs Routledge,' Rathbone concluded, 'you have a six months' notice to quit the premises. Here is the document. Redevelopment commences in January. And now I must say good-bye and thank you so much for your kind hospitality.'

'I'm afraid you must have made a mistake!' Mrs Routledge hardly recognized her own voice, it was so deep and gracious and seemed to match exactly the panels of brocade and elegant French antique furniture now ranged against the walls of the salon. 'My name is Lady Kitty Carson, you know. I believe we have had the pleasure?'

At this point Cridge came up with a sparkling glass dish containing almonds. Mrs Routledge saw to her amazement that he wore tails and a white tie so clean and starched that it looked like an invitation card freshly laid around his neck; his hair was shining and carefully combed, with a side parting that gave him an almost military air. So miracles were possible after all! In her haze of gratitude, Mrs Routledge reflected that the Lord was good: you only had to pray for something long enough and it was yours. She bit into an almond and was repaid by a twinge of pain from one of Lady Kitty's unknown cavities. Despite this she continued to smile coquettishly up at Mr Rathbone, an epigram ready and waiting on her lips and all the grandeur and magnificence of the apartments giving her the confidence she had so long needed to capture this elusive man.

'My dear Lady Kitty!' Mr Poynter was at her side, and with him Mrs Houghton. It seemed that the change in the party had brought the couple together again – Mrs Houghton's arm was linked with Mr Poynter's – and a gold band gleamed on her fourth finger. Only Miss Scranton, who was still in the dowdy clothes of the Westringham party, glowered over by the kitchen door; and Johnny and Melinda, anxious to talk confidentially to their author, did not appear sufficiently appreciative of the evening their hostess was giving. She turned her smile on Mr

Poynter – and as Mr Poynter was becoming increasingly obsequious, the first signs of flattery and gallant manners appeared obligingly on Mr Rathbone. He shrank a little, as if to show he no longer thought himself larger than anyone else in the room; he took his hand, which had been jingling small change in his pocket in an insolent manner, sharply away from it, as if to show he would only play with notes of big denomination in future, if he played with money in the presence of a lady at all; his teeth spread out across his lower jaw in the semblance of a carnivore come at last face to face with his prey. Mrs Routledge shuddered in anticipation, and spoke directly to Mr Poynter.

'I'm so terribly glad you could come! Unfortunately, there is a nasty thunder storm brewing up, or we could have had drinks in the garden. But never mind!'

Cridge chuckled at this, giving the impression that his mistress had been witty again, and a low murmur of laughter passed from Mr Poynter to Mrs Houghton and on to Mr Rathbone. Mrs Routledge bridled, and then looked modest.

'I'd like you to meet my bride, Lady Kitty. This thunder has indeed plagued the day.' Mr Poynter nodded meaningfully and Mrs Houghton joined in. 'Our wedding was almost spoiled by it, you know!'

Miss Briggs came up to her hostess and held out her hand. She was in evening dress but not, Mrs Routledge was thankful to note, with accompanying sash and garter. Could it really be true that sanity had returned to the Westringham, that Miss Briggs no longer thought she was the monarch, that Mrs Houghton would triumph over the disgusting Miss Scranton and Cridge would remain a paragon of cleanliness and humility? Mrs Routledge wiped away a tear with a monogrammed handkerchief and beamed at the newly married couple.

'Many congratulations!'

'A marriage late in life. I consider that very beautiful,' Mr Rathbone said. Mrs Routledge felt his eyes bore into her profile and she simpered. 'I lost my dear wife some time ago, and I dream always of finding a true mate, a replacement for something that can never be replaced, and yet, one never knows . . .'

'Mrs Houghton,' Melinda said loudly, stepping up to the

154

novelist bride and taking her by the arm. 'Johnny and I want to talk to you. To come to some compromise . . .'

'Here is Her Majesty,' Miss Briggs breathed. 'Oh, doesn't she look wonderful tonight?'

Mrs Routledge flinched. Cridge was standing by the tall panelled door and he was bowing low. A hush fell over the room and Mr Rathbone stood back, encircling Mrs Routledge's waist with his arm as he did so. A mixture of emotions conflicted in Mrs Routledge. If she really was Lady Kitty, then she could greet the Queen and the party would be remembered as the most successful she had ever thrown. Mr Rathbone would almost certainly propose and they would live happily ever after in this delightful house. Only Miss Scranton and the scruffy-looking characters Mrs Houghton seemed to have invited would find their dreams unrealized – and not everyone can have what they want all the time. But Mrs Routledge was not quite sure of herself yet. Suppose, on her way over to the door, the walls of the Westringham dining-room made themselves apparent again . . . suppose, as she made her low curtsy, the smell of the basement came up to meet her nostrils – and those of her sovereign – and the greasy door handle, clasped in Cridge's filthy hand, was the first thing she saw on coming up from her obeisance. Or to find, on looking shyly into the Queen's eyes, the unworthy gaze of Miss Briggs . . . Mrs Routledge was cautious by now; and contented herself with writhing delicately in Mr Rathbone's embrace, waiting for events to unfurl themselves, for Lady Kitty's house to remain as it was and not sink back into the Westringham just at the moment of her glory and her power.

'Her Majesty the Queen!' said Cridge in a loud announcer's voice.

'Please, Mrs Houghton,' said Melinda. 'We've no time to lose over this!'

Lady Kitty's drawing-room held steady as Cridge led the monarch over to Mrs Routledge and retired in deference from the meeting. The chandelier seemed to throw a stronger, richer light, the brocade panels could now be seen to be hung with Old Masters – though Mrs Routledge, in the second's flash she had of them before going down into her curtsy, was appalled by the hideous, disfigured faces of the great portraits – a sofa upholstered in cherry velvet appeared at a convenient distance and was clearly where Her Majesty would hope to sit when the introductions were over. Miss Briggs greeted the Queen with soft reverential familiarity. Mr Rathbone bowed and was told in the sweetest tones that the knighthood, although performed under difficult circumstances (the thunder was blamed again here) was perfectly valid and that he was Sir Geoffrey for all the world to know. Mr Poynter – and this was odd, Mrs Routledge thought – welcomed the Queen to his City and said he hoped she would find herself comfortable in her new quarters; Mrs Houghton affirmed this, expressed her pleasure at having so august a neighbour; and invited the Queen and Miss Briggs to tea on Wednesday week. Mrs Routledge began to feel a little confused and worried, but reminded herself that things were going better for her than they ever had before, and she mustn't complain if Mr Poynter and Mrs Houghton's snobbery had got rather out of hand for the time being. She settled on a hardbacked chair near the monarch and awaited her turn to make conversation, while Mrs Houghton, she was glad to see, was in the process of telling her two unwanted guests to leave the party, and at once. The only strange thing, Mrs Routledge thought, was the language she used; but it seemed to be having the desired effect, and the travel-stained characters stood pale in front of the author, both clearly on the point of leaving Lady Kitty's house for good.

'She went and threw herself on her bed,' Mrs Houghton spat at them as they stood immobile before her. 'She wept, she knew she could no longer live like this. Johnny came in once and she looked up at him in mute appeal, but he continued to throw his possessions into his suitcase . . . the shared tissue of their life together . . . the sacred objects . . . she scooped the pills from the bottle and pressed them into her mouth. Johnny left, doors slammed all over the house as he went, as if a strong wind had got up and was blowing him from her forever . . . on the shores of a distant lake she saw him standing before she went down for the last time, the haze from the drug came purple over her eyelids . . . Good-bye Johnny . . . Good-bye . . .

'*The End*,' Mrs Houghton said snappily when she had finished.

'Now are you both satisfied? I have better things to do than plan out your futures for the rest of my life I can assure you. Now be off – and I don't want to see you again.' She leaned forward and began to engage the Queen in animated conversation, and Mrs Routledge nodded with pleasure at the sight of the bedraggled suicide and her boyfriend going dejectedly from the room. Now there was only Miss Scranton to dispose of – and a quick glance at Miss Scranton's corner showed that the schoolmistress seemed to be reaching the end of her tether and should be dealt with fast. She was sitting astride her chair and her bare thighs and legs – most unsuitable for meeting the Queen, and Mrs Routledge had the uncomfortable feeling that if they were all to find themselves suddenly in the Westringham again it would be due to Miss Scranton's scandalous appearance – were thickly coated with damp sand; her hair seemed to have grown longer and thicker, and her eyes, wild and staring, were fixed on the sycophantic backs of Mr Poynter and his bride. Mrs Routledge cleared her throat and rose nervously. Skirting the recumbent figure of Marcus Tapp (she hoped the Queen had not seen him, but certainly no mention had been made of the irregularity of an evening spent in the presence of a sleeping revolutionary and republican), she went over to Miss Scranton and asked her politely if she had had everything she wanted at the party. Enough to drink? Had she tried the mouth-watering little canapés? Appearing at Mrs Routledge's side, the angelic Cridge handed plates, and a salver laden with glasses of champagne. But Miss Scranton made no answer, her eyes only seemed to grow wider and more mournful, and Mrs Routledge decided to take a firmer line.

'I'm afraid I have to ask you to go, Miss Scranton. This is a salon, you understand, and we encourage elegant conversation. I fear you must be at the wrong party, Miss Scranton.'

Just as with the other events in Mrs Routledge's miraculous evening, she had only to wish something for it to come true at once. Miss Scranton rose, and like a sleepwalker made for the door, which Cridge ran ahead to hold open for her. She did not look back once, and when she had gone Mrs Routledge found herself catching the eye of the Queen. A gleam of relief could be detected there. Now Tapp must be carried out into the street, and

157

it would be a perfect party. Mrs Routledge made her way back to the little nucleus round the monarch and sat down demurely, hands folded. Mr Rathbone was ending a discourse on money and his audience was listening to him with the rapt, distracted expressions sometimes found on the faces of music lovers when a great concert is drawing to a close. Mrs Routledge assumed this expression, and dreamed of her marriage to the financial genius, the town mansion where they would live in the season and the hunting box where they would spend the crisp autumns and romantic, snowy winters. She was glad her old abode, the Westringham, was due for demolition: it was clear that Mr Rathbone had no intention of allowing her to return to that squalid place, and would be quite masterful in his choice of their new home.

'So we must adopt the index system – as in Brazil for instance,' Mr Rathbone was saying. 'You may reply, Your Majesty, that Brazil is an under-developed country and we are not, but unless we peg prices and incomes . . .'

The first peal of thunder sounded above the house. Mrs Routledge, trying to conceal it – there was something crude and uninvited about the sound – coughed and tittered loudly. Mrs Houghton turned to her with an air of concern.

'Don't you love thunder, Lady Kitty? I always think it's one of the few real reminders of Nature we get nowadays. So strong, so refreshing!'

'Of course, of course,' said Mrs Routledge quickly, as Mr Rathbone broke off his talk and looked inquiringly up, as if to find the source of the thunder in the chandelier (which was, rather worryingly, swaying: Mrs Routledge wondered if something terrible was happening upstairs – Miss Scranton's madness, or a battle between Mrs Houghton's unwanted guests). Another peal followed, and then another. Miss Briggs gasped, and covered her cowardice by calling Cridge and asking for more champagne for the monarch. Mr Poynter rose to his feet, divested himself of his dinner jacket and threw it on the floor in front of the Royal Personage, as if expecting the inevitable downpour to flood into Lady Kitty's rooms; and Mrs Routledge, remembering her role as anxious hostess, ran to the window, pulled aside the heavy damask curtains and looked out. When she saw what she saw she screamed. And in the ensuing confusion Marcus Tapp woke, to find Rathbone and Poynter trampling over his legs and a woman who appeared to be the Queen of his country staring at him with icy disapproval. The lights in the chandelier went out and the whole glassy contraption fell to the ground. A stunned silence was succeeded by a babble of hysterical sound. Rathbone was the first to recover his composure, and a commanding voice rang out in Lady Kitty's uncertain drawing-room.

'Everyone keep their heads! An explanation must be found for all this. First, what is that crowd doing out there? And secondly, where the devil are we? My apologies for the language, Ma'am.'

'Excuse me.' Mr Poynter sounded faint and frightened in comparison. 'But if I may . . . this is my City, you see . . . I recognize these streets . . . at the back of HQ, yes that's where we are. Not Lady Kitty's part of the City at all . . . I'm afraid I simply can't understand that at all . . .'

'The back of HQ? Now what's the man talking about?' Mr Rathbone demanded tersely. 'Is he dreaming or something? These crowds don't look too happy to me. Better go out and see what they want!'

'No!' Mrs Routledge reached out a protective arm in spite of herself. 'You might get hurt, Mr Rathbone!'

'If this is Mr Poynter's City,' the Queen made herself heard for the first time, 'then he should deal with the insurrection. Mr Poynter, what are you going to do about this state of affairs?'

At this point the thunder reached deafening proportions. The windows blew open and a gust of crowd air and rain came in on the guests. Mr Poynter ran from the room and opened a window, leaning out and then going in again like a weatherman. The crowd gave a low roar and then fell back into its placid, expectant quiet. Mr Poynter reappeared in the salon, stumbling amongst the unfamiliar furniture (for upstairs had been strangely like his bedroom at the Westringham, and he had expected, instinctively, to come down to the bulging cupboard and rickety tables of the dining-room). Lightning streaked across the sky outside. The atmospheric pressure of the two great masses – the crowds in the black streets gathered and breathing and waiting, and the lunging, heavy clouds above – were intolerable by now, and Miss Briggs went down in a dead faint without a warning murmur. It was while she was being tended by the Queen and Mrs Routledge, her boned dress loosened and the modest tiara taken carefully from her head, that Marcus Tapp ran to the window, leapt out and disappeared into the crowd. A shout went up from Rathbone and Poynter, but he had gone. Trembling, Mr Poynter closed the windows and addressed the guests in the collapsing city of his dreams.

'This is a state of emergency, Your Majesty, ladies and gentlemen. The escape of that ruffian may mean a civil war too terrible to contemplate. And,' he peered round the darkened room and his voice grew shrill, 'and Miss Scranton? Where is she?'

'I sent her away,' Mrs Routledge said. 'She was spoiling the party, Mr Poynter!'

'You fool! so she's loose too!' Poynter's shoulders sagged and for a moment he looked an aged man, outlined against the window and the waiting crowd and the harsh light from the street lamps. His new bride shrank from him, and it was Mrs Routledge's task to put out a comforting hand.

'We must prepare for disaster,' he continued when the despair had partly passed. 'We must hide in the cellar and hope for a merciful end.'

'Certainly not!' the Queen put in at this point.

Outside a low moan went up from the people. The eyes of Mr Poynter's victims went reluctantly to the sky above the crowd, and a shocked murmur ran round the remains of Lady Kitty's party, even Cridge expressing surprise and wonderment at the apparitions to be seen now the thunder clouds had rolled back. The cloud women straddled the heavens. Their warlike, wispy faces stared down, it seemed, right into the room; their eyes, balls of indigo vapour, glowered in terrible accusations. Shafts from their cirrus bows shot across the dark backdrop and made wide girdles round the moon. Then the thick mass of cloud moved over them once more and they were obscured from view. The crowd let out a thunderous sigh. Miss Briggs struggled back to consciousness and demanded to be told what she had missed. Mr Poynter opened his mouth to explain, and was silent.

'We must mend the lights in here,' said Mr Rathbone after a pause. 'My dear Kitty, perhaps you would ask your manservant to conduct me to the fusebox.'

Mr Poynter, encouraged by this show of common sense, drew the curtains back into place; the fusebox was found and the lights mended; and as Mrs Routledge had known, had dreaded and prayed against as the men fiddled with the fuses in the dark and the rain began to fall more heavily, what sprang into sight at the touch of the switch was of course not Lady Kitty Carson's at all, but the Westringham: the Westringham in all its dinginess and dilapidation, the dining-room already dripping from the ceiling where once the chandelier had been, the cut glass droplets replaced by muddy water; the grease-marked walls, the smell of Cridge's basement strong and fetid in the hot and rainy weather. The bulging cupboard seemed to laugh widemouthed at Mrs Routledge and her pretensions. The Queen was on an unsteady chair now, by the basement steps, and her head low in a handkerchief. Mrs Houghton let out an exclamation. Mrs Routledge sank on to the chair normally occupied by Mr Poynter, and stared helplessly at her guests. As if the recent interlude had passed already from his memory, Mr Rathbone approached her and held out his document, glancing at the same time impatiently at his watch.

'Notice to quit the premises within six months,' he finished off. 'And now, as I said before, dear lady . . .'

'Lady Kitty?' warbled Mrs Routledge. But she knew she was as good as done for. Her own cheap dress with the large cameo brooch rose up to meet her eye from the heaving bosom below. A plastic fern in a plastic vase trembled on the table by her hand. The closed curtains, against which Mr Poynter stood with a troubled expression, were thin and worn and an all-too-familiar safety pin protruded from the drooping hem. Mrs Routledge tried to catch his eye but Mr Poynter looked away from her. He was staring desperately at Mr Rathbone, as if the financier was the only person present capable of restoring the elegance of the past hour. Yet, in turn, Mr Rathbone seemed extremely anxious to leave.

'Many thanks for your kind hospitality.' He bowed, went into the hall and stepped out through the front door while the others, defeated, watched him go. But then he stopped, and could be seen to make a mopping motion in the direction of his brow. For if the interior of the Westringham had been restored to its rightful proportions, the outside world had indubitably changed since he had been in there. Mr Poynter's City – and this time he could not count it as an hallucination, the product of a tiring day, the emotions natural to a man on receiving a knighthood – lay before him. The crowds were dispersing a little, but a thin shout of animosity went up when he was spotted on the doorstep. He retired, and closed the door behind him, stood facing the intolerable imposters in the dining-room of the property he planned shortly to topple to the ground.

'What is the meaning of this?' Mr Rathbone asked in a severe tone.

Mr Poynter walked slowly up to him. His face was chalk white and his legs shaking, but Rathbone felt no pity for the man.

'It's because they've got out.' His voice was scarcely more than a wheeze; to Mr Rathbone's irritation hearing what he said involved stooping down to his now greatly reduced level.

'Who's got out? Is this a zoo or what?'

Cridge, tattered once more and immeasurably filthy, gave a low laugh just to the left of where Mr Rathbone was standing.

'He means the Scranton and that young fellow,' he cleared up the point. 'Till we catch them we won't have any peace tonight I fear.'

Mr Poynter, despite his revulsion for Cridge, nodded agreement. The dreams had escaped; they were trapped in a pool of reality; standing there, in front of the man he most respected, he must do the one thing he most despised, the ultimate in rudeness and contempt: he must close his eyes and sleep. His eyelids went down. Cridge could be heard with his laugh again. Mr Rathbone strode up to Mr Poynter and shook him by the shoulder.

'What the hell d'you think you're doing, man? This is no time for sleep, for God's sake!'

But as he spoke a strange drowsiness came over Mr Rathbone. It spread across his head and down into his chest and made his legs heavy and incapable of movement. For a few seconds he struggled manfully against the sensation. He saw the Queen asleep, her head on the soup-stained tablecloth, the last recipient of Miss Scranton's nervous eating habits – he saw Mrs Routledge and Miss Briggs sleeping on their feet, with oddly contented expressions as if they had been rescued from the pain of a nightmare; he saw Mrs Houghton, her crocodile bag held out before her like a trophy, asleep in a rigid formal pose as if she had turned all of a sudden into a mannequin in a shop window. Mr Rathbone let his lids come down on his cheekbones.

Marcus Tapp, in his waking dream, wandered the streets of Mr Poynter's disintegrating city. His instincts and his training told him to make for the radio stations and the water supply, but his legs took him at a slow pace through the wide boulevards of the residential quarter, the crooked lanes of the ghetto and the monumental architecture of the main square; and his eye registered all he saw with a kind of dim recognition, as if the pattern of the city had been at some early stage implanted in his brain. The arcades, the wide portals of the grand houses, the steep, arbitrary twists and turns of the poor region were all somehow familiar to him, and just as familiar to him were his future actions: he wandered, but with foreknowledge of his destination, like a tourist exploring the city for the second time.

Rain was falling steadily, but Marcus was impervious to it. He saw that some of the buildings were succumbing already to the downpour: portions of grey stone façades had detached themselves from the main edifice, had turned to sodden papier mâché and were lying in the gutters, where they melted gradually to pulp and were washed with the rushing water into the drains; a part of Mr Poynter's headquarters – the balcony, in fact, and the french windows behind it – had broken off and melted, and were stepped over by soldiers at drill in the courtyard as if they were no more than drenched ribbons of black paper; parts of the ghetto were coming down to form soft barricades in the narrow streets. He must hurry, if his task was to be accomplished before the city disappeared altogether, leaving nothing but a perishable ruin behind it; at the preordained moment, when the tour of the precincts had been made and the signs of recent warfare in the garden of Mr Poynter's residence noted, Marcus felt his legs quicken under him, his shoulders make an about turn in the wall of rain which

164

encased his body. He went with a sure step to the industrial zone and marched into the biggest factory. The crowds, sheltering in the precarious doorways along his route, gave a ragged cheer as he went. An unearthly light had replaced the street lamps and pools of darkness of west London, it was as if dawn and twilight had become confused, and if there was to be a day ahead it would contain only the blank certainty of night. In this aura of limited promise the crowds stood like ghosts, and Marcus passed between them upright behind his pane of water.

The Revolution went according to Marcus's plan. Factories were occupied, and there was fighting with Mr Poynter's troops; the workers were victorious. HQ was stormed and Mr Poynter taken prisoner, his hands tied behind his scarlet-coated back and his eyes blindfolded in readiness for public execution. In the Stock Exchange where Mr Rathbone was shouting and gesticulating like a marionette pulled on ever-tightening wires – the sense of his connection with the deep bedrock gone, he was twitched from above now rather than connected with the base – the money was destroyed and Rathbone himself murdered, his body flung out on to the slush of the streets. Mrs Houghton, presiding at a literary luncheon, was bound and gagged and left to sit there indefinitely with her respectful and terrified admirers. The Queen and Miss Briggs, mere figureheads, were shown compassion by Marcus and expelled from the fast-melting walls of the city, to wander in permanent exile amongst the replicas of Stonehenge and the plaster cast of Windsor Castle. Mrs Routledge and Cridge, obsequious and subservient to Marcus as they were, were put to work in the great kitchens of the once noble houses, preparing soup for the forces of liberation. The city was taken – but it was disappearing fast! There was so little time to lose, if a new state was to be built on the foundations of the old – and Marcus lacked the imagination to start anew – so little time, when even as Mrs Routledge stirred the pot the walls of the kitchen buckled and sagged with rain, when the railings of the courtyard where Mr Poynter was to be executed drooped and swayed like sodden matches, when the crenellated walls of the city were breaking down and the accumulated rainwater outside was pouring in to cause yet more confusion. Marcus made his plans and shouted orders. Men were sent to the surrounding countryside to cut wood, so that a simple temporary city should stand while the perfect state of the future was under way. It was while he was marching on this mission at the head of his bedraggled troops – and it was hard to march now: the cardboard streets had become a treacherous mire, the men sinking in thick, wet paper up to their shins as they went – that Marcus first espied the women; they strode from every angle down the wide avenues; they carried shields and spears and they were twice the size of the men; strange, incomprehensible war-songs poured from them as they advanced.

The battle was brief and bitter. The men were armed and the bullets killed the women; Marcus saw Miss Scranton go down clasping her side; matted hair and severed, gigantic limbs were strewn on the dissolving streets. But despite their victory, the men were shaken by the fight and Marcus led them back to the now faintly delineated courtyard in order to raise their spirits with an execution. Mr Poynter was tied to a post. The squad faced him. Shots rang out in the just visible remains of the city. Mr Poynter's head lolled against the post. As Marcus stood watching, a smile of triumph on his lips, the rain stopped and in the improved but still uncertain light the crowds began to drag themselves from the sodden streets and out into the area which had once been beyond the walls. Marcus called to them, but they did not look back or answer. Soon he was left alone, in a devastated waste of pulp and dying bodies.

Epilogue

Mr Poynter woke suddenly at what sounded like pistol shots going off. Of course – it was only Mrs Routledge with the early morning tea – but he was surprised to find himself fully dressed on his bed, as if someone had lain him out there when he was drunk. He took the tea gratefully and sipped it; and as he did so reflected that he had had a particularly bad night. Mrs Routledge still lingered in the doorway, and from the adjoining rooms came the familiar sounds of Miss Scranton washing herself prudishly and Miss Briggs stamping down her heel into a walking shoe. Further on, Mrs Houghton was already pounding at her typewriter. Mr Poynter smiled feebly up at his landlady, and remarked it had been very heavy rain for the time of year.

'And that's not all!' Mrs Routledge whisked Mr Rathbone's document from her pocket and handed it to the only male resident of the Westringham (she did not count Cridge as such).

'This arrived this morning, Mr Poynter. Who would have thought it? Tonight was to have been the night of our party, you know. I shall certainly cancel the invitation now.'

Poynter reached for his glasses. He read the document carefully. His hands began to tremble as his eyes went over the small print, and he let out a groan of fear.

'But where are we all to go then, Mrs Routledge? This is monstrous. We must take this up with the authorities . . .'

'Mr Rathbone *is* the authorities,' Mrs Routledge replied. 'It breaks my heart Mr Poynter, it really does. But I felt I must inform the clients at the earliest possible opportunity.' She squared her shoulders and sighed. 'I shall be going into retirement at Eastbourne, Mr Poynter. My days of running an establishment are over now!'

'But surely there is something we can do about this?' Mr

Poynter, his security running out from under him, raised himself in the bed and set his mind racing. 'What about Mrs Houghton? Doesn't she have connections?' (He had a dim memory of some unpleasantness with Mrs Houghton lately, but he was not awake enough yet to remember. At any rate, she would be as keen as he was to save the Westringham from demolition.)

'Mrs Houghton is returning to Knightsbridge,' Mrs Routledge replied. 'She has lost a close relative, I gather.'

'Oh dear, I'm so sorry!'

'If you ask me, it's a good thing.' Mrs Routledge lowered her voice and half closed the door behind her. A stench rose from the hall, and Poynter recollected it was Thursday, the day Cridge emptied his pots. He buried his nose in his sheet and looked wonderingly up at Mrs Routledge as she stood over him.

'She keeps saying she can get this person back if she types long enough,' Mrs Routledge confided. 'Not quite right in the . . . you know what I mean. And Miss Scranton's not well today so she has to have hot water instead of tea. If you ask me, Mr Poynter, I'm well out of the hotel business. With the exception of yourself of course. Well you've never been any trouble, I must say!'

'What's wrong with Miss Scranton?' asked Mr Poynter, feeling again that unaccountable sinking of the heart. 'Usually the picture of health, isn't she?'

'Indigestion. Complains of a pain in the side.' Mrs Routledge put her hand on the doorknob and made preparations to leave.

'And Miss Briggs is going to Persia for an indefinite visit,' she said in a loud undertone as she pulled the door ajar. 'Says she's been invited by the Shah, but you never can tell!'

With this, Mrs Routledge was gone. Mr Poynter lay on in bed, digesting the news. Downstairs he could hear Mrs Routledge telling Cridge to clean out the kitchens, his refusal to do this, and the ping of the telephone as Mrs Routledge made her call.

'Mr Rathbone? Oh I'm so sorry to disturb you at home, Mr Rathbone, before you go to the office, but I'm a teeny weeny bit surprised at the document I received this morning. What's that? Oh well of course one would love to have the opportunity to discuss . . .'

There was a pause, and in this time Mr Poynter shifted un-

168

comfortably under the bedclothes, fragments of unwelcome memory returning to him as he did so. He felt uneasy and insecure and depressed. There had been something once which had sustained him through the days, and he had now a feeling of inconsolable loss, as if whatever it was had gone from him for ever. He thought of his wife; but all that had been too long ago to return to him now with such fresh grief. As Mrs Routledge resumed her conversation below, Mr Poynter concluded that it must be the knowledge of having to move oneself, go off to a new and strange hotel, that was unsettling him like that. At his age moving was not to be taken lightly. And his bad dreams of the past few nights had no doubt been some premonition of this future insecurity. He reached for his cup of tea and drained it to the dregs.

'Well of course I'd simply love it if you came!' Mrs Routledge was saying into the telephone in the hall. 'I do understand, Mr Rathbone, one can't keep redundant buildings standing just for sentimental reasons! Good ... well about six-thirty then. How simply perfect!'

She rang off and began to question Cridge about nuts and tonic water. Wearily, Mr Poynter rose and dressed. He heard Miss Scranton march past on her way down to the dining-room. Miss Briggs followed. Feeling his years, Mr Poynter went shakily out on to the landing, passed the room where Mrs Houghton was typing, and descended into the cleaner air of a Thursday morning in the Westringham.

More About Penguins
and Pelicans

The Midas Consequence

Michael Ayrton

In a restaurant in the south of France, an old Italian sculptor holds court. He has climbed to the pinnacle of his art, received the bounty of the gods; all he touches turns to gold.

'There are flickers of thunder and bursts of lightning, and real myth horror ... this is one of the few novels about an artist which rings true, and rings with a drama which will still clang in the reader's mind long after he has finished' – *Books and Bookmen*

'Mr Ayrton is a writer of rare creativity and constant fascination' – *Sunday Telegraph*

Women in the Wall

Julia O'Faolain

Away from the chaos, violence and flames of sixth-century Gaul, the nuns lead their quiet lives as Brides of Christ. For Radegunda retreat means sainthood and mystic mortifications. Sweet Abbess Agnes tends the garden.

But the world crashes harshly into this citadel of quiet. The light of peace is guttering all across Gaul, and the convent is plunged into barbaric night.

'Supple and stark, urbane and anguished ... abounds with life and dry comment. If only for the vitality coaxed from the fog of history, it is an adventure to read' – Christopher Wordsworth in the *Guardian*

The Distance and the Dark

Terence de Vere White

Until the murder of his son, Everard Harvey had kept an open mind about the Irish troubles. But faced with a failing marriage, his own guilt and lack of cooperation from the law, he is forced to do something; something that he knows will lead to tragedy.

Terence de Vere White brilliantly interweaves private desires and despairs with the terrible problems of a country racked with subversive political violence.

'Wit, tolerance and Olympian mischief ... Terence de Vere White has shown again that he is one of the most sophisticated and cultivated of our writers' – *Irish Press*

Foreign Affairs

Sean O'Faolain

'The finest collection of stories to come out of Ireland for many years' – *Hibernia*

Eight stories from the acknowledged master of Irish letters. They deal in love and strangeness, from Dublin to Brussels to the crumbled remains of ancient Sybaris, delineating with wit and colour the silent spaces between lovers.

'There is in these tales a freshness, an absence of nostalgia, and a quality of curiosity that packs a different kind of surprise into every one' – *Sunday Telegraph*

The Conservationist

Nadine Gordimer

'A triumph of style ... this is a novel of enormous
power' – Paul Theroux in the *New Statesman*

Mehring is rich. He has all that white privilege in South
Africa can give him. Isolated, at once cold and passionate,
he challenges history in his determination that nothing
shall change his way of life.

But Africa cannot be bought by the white man, now.

'One of those rare works of literature that command the
special respect reserved for artistic daring and fulfilled
ambition' – Paul Bailey in the *Observer*

No Place Like: Selected Stories

Nadine Gordimer

'A magnificent collection worthy of all homage' – Graham
Greene in the *Observer* Books of the Year 1976.

With this collection of thirty-one stories Nadine Gordimer
displays all her descriptive power and acute insight,
pinning Africa to the page like a butterfly for our
inspection.

'This dazzlingly rich, impressively solid selection ... The
scrupulous intensity of her regard shouts from the opening
sentences' – Valentine Cunningham in the *New Statesman*

'To read these stories in their chronological order is to
absorb what has been happening in South Africa over the
years ... This volume is one not to be missed by anyone
who cares for real writing' – Elizabeth Berridge in the
Daily Telegraph

The Crack

Emma Tennant

Look!
Look what's happened!
A crack has opened in the Thames!
Hampstead uplifted high in the sky!

Watch the turmoil spread. See the loony psychoanalysts lead their demented flock around the cracked and broken streets. A religious maniac's at large, she's promising her female believers a new and Manless life on the 'Other Side'.

And through it all goes Baba; dear, sweet, kind, unliberated Baba, leaving a trail of love and destruction in her wake.

'How stimulating prophecies of catastrophe are ...'
– George Hill in *The Times*

'Lewis Carroll technique applied to H. G. Wells material ... as a comic apocalypse this novel could hardly be bettered!' – *The Times Literary Supplement*

Originally published as *The Time of the Crack*